CREATED BY

NORM HARPER & LOUIE JOYCE

LETTERED BY

OCEANO RANSFORD

For SH,
We are the luckiest.
—NH

For Dashi & Shug.
—LJ

OKAY, I'LL QUIZ YOU. WHAT'S THIS?
HORSESHOE.
AND IT'S GOOD LUCK BECAUSE...?

IT HAS SEVEN NAIL HOLES.
AND?

IT'S LIKE THE MOON... UH, WHAT'S IT...
...CRESCENT SHAPED?
BINGO.

WHAT'S THIS ONE?
THOSE ARE MY FAVORITE--
THE FISHHOOKS.

FISHHOOKS ARE LUCKY?
NOT ACTUAL HOOKS, NO. THIS MEANS TWO JACKS. LIKE IN CARDS.
YOU UNDERSTAND?
UH-HUH.
OVER A HUNDRED YEARS AGO, YOUR GREAT-GREAT GRANDDAD ZANE PLAYED CARDS. FOR A LIVING.

THE FISHHOOKS WERE ZANE'S LUCKY CARDS. WHENEVER ZANE HAD AT LEAST TWO JACKS IN HIS HAND, HE WON.
AND THAT LUCK MADE HIM FAMOUS THROUGHOUT THE WILD WEST. ZANE 'FISHHOOKS' MILLS WAS A LEGEND.
HE EVEN WORE A SYMBOL OF THEM AROUND HIS NECK. TO SHOW OFF AND INTIMIDATE THE OTHER PLAYERS.
IF FISHHOOKS MILLS WAS SITTING ACROSS THE TABLE, YOU HAD TO BE READY TO PLAY THE BEST GAME OF YOUR LIFE.

SO HE NEVER LOST?
ALL GAMBLERS LOSE NOW AND AGAIN. AND IF ZANE WASN'T DEALT HIS LUCKY CARDS, HE WAS JUST ANOTHER GAMBLER.
BUT WHENEVER HE GOT DEALT THE FISHHOOKS, IT WAS LIKE MAGIC.
HE WAS INVINCIBLE.
UNTIL ONE DAY...
...ZANE'S LUCKY CARDS FAILED HIM.
AND WITH THAT HAND, ZANE LOST EVERYTHING.

ZANE'S WIFE AND CHILDREN WERE USED TO UPS AND DOWNS, WINS AND LOSSES.

BUT THEY'D NEVER KNOWN A DOWN THAT LOW BEFORE. IT WAS THE LAST STRAW.

WITH NOTHING LEFT TO THEM BUT THE CLOTHES ON THEIR BACKS AND THE DEED TO THEIR LAND, THEY THREW ZANE OUT.

AND SO ZANE WENT OFF IN SEARCH OF LADY LUCK HERSELF, TO ASK HER WHY HIS HOOKS HAD FAILED HIM.

DID HE FIND HER?

HE MUST'VE...

...BECAUSE NOT LONG AFTER HE DISAPPEARED, THE WIFE AND CHILDREN HE LEFT BEHIND DISCOVERED OIL ON THEIR LAND.

AND THAT MADE THE MILLS FAMILY INTO MILLIONAIRES.

OH GOOD, OUR DAUGHTER IS STILL AWAKE.
MOM!

SHOULD I PUT ON SOME COFFEE? YOU KNOW THE PEDIATRICIAN SAID SHE'S NOT GETTING ENOUGH ESPRESSO IN HER DIET.

IT'S TRUE. NINE OUT OF TEN DOCTORS AGREE THAT SLEEP IS FOR THE WEAK.
WE MUST KEEP OUR CHILDREN UP AT ALL HOURS TO TEST THEIR FORTITUDE.
ONLY THE STRONGEST SHALL INHERIT MY LANDS AND TITLES.

YOUR OFFICE JUST CALLED. THE ALARM'S GOING OFF, AND THEY NEED YOUR SECURITY KEY TO RESET IT.
FIRST MY GAME GETS RAINED OUT, NOW THIS. I GUESS ZANE FELL ASLEEP ON HIS WATCH TONIGHT.
TICKLE

AND YOU SHOULD FOLLOW SUIT.
KISS

LEAVE THE BAT? I WANT TO STUDY SOME MORE.
YOUR MOM'S RIGHT. YOU NEED TO SLEEP.
I CAN STUDY WHILE I SLEEP. PLEASE?

OKAY. ZANE CAN WATCH OVER YOU TONIGHT. BUT DON'T LET HIM CATCH YOU AWAKE.

GROSS, YOU'RE GONNA LET HER SLEEP WITH THAT THING?

-CLICK
IT DOES COMPLEMENT THE MUD YOU GOT ALL OVER HER COMFORTER.
MAYBE I SHOULD JUST SEW HER A TEDDY BEAR OUT OF YOUR DIRTY SOCKS?

SO MELODRAMATIC. SHE'LL BE FINE.

EMER

To Raveng

Seamróg
Castle

Luchorborough

Gealach
River

Clochtooth
Ranges

Clover Farms

Rocky Ruins

A HISTORY
OF HAPHAVEN

BY SMIDGEN STONEWICK

Chapter 1

HAPHAVEN
Slugwood forest
Salt Mines
Badgercragg Mountains

Five years later.

MILLS! YOU'RE UP.

ON IT!
HEY, HEY, HEY-- HOLD UP!

WE TALKED ABOUT THIS. ALUMINUM BAT DURING LEAGUE PLAY. TAKE IT.
TRYING TO JINX ME, COACH?

MILLS, THAT WAS NOT A REQUEST!
ALEX!

STRIKE ONE!
SWING
SWISH

LET'S GO, ALEX!
Whoooo!

STRIKE TWO!

Come on, Zane. Help me out here.
Wherever you are, wake up and pay attention.

CRACK

HOME RUN!
Yes! Thank you, Zane!

GREAT JOB OUT THERE TODAY.
THANKS.
DID YOU GET A CHANCE TO TALK TO THE TEAM ABOUT THE PARTY?

Ugh, again with the stupid party.
I JUST DON'T WANT TO MAKE A FUSS THIS YEAR.
WE MADE A FUSS LAST YEAR.

DOESN'T HAVE TO BE A BIG DEAL. MAYBE WE COULD JUST TAKE TWO OR THREE OF YOUR FRIENDS OUT FOR A FANCY DINNER? STEAK AND LOBSTER?
NO ENTRY
LEAVE IT ALONE, MOM.

IT'S JUST A NUMBER, ALEX.
YOU SURVIVED BEING THIRTEEN DAYS AND THIRTEEN WEEKS AND THIRTEEN MONTHS, AND EVERY DAY THOUSANDS OF KIDS MIRACULOUSLY MANAGE TO SURVIVE INTO THEIR FOURTEENTH YEAR.

Well, thousands of kids aren't as jinxed as I am.

COACH ASKED YOU TO USE A DIFFERENT BAT, DIDN'T HE?
I SAW HIM TRY TO HAND IT TO YOU.

YEAH, BUT... GAME-WINNING HOME RUN.
Where's the toy?
I DIDN'T LET YOU JOIN THE LEAGUE JUST TO WIN BASEBALL GAMES.
SHOULD'VE SIGNED ME UP FOR BOWLING.
CHOMP
CHOMP
CHOMP

BOWLING?
YEAH, IF YOU DIDN'T WANT ME WINNING BASEBALL GAMES, YOU SHOULD'VE...
Forget it.

I DON'T WANT YOU TO TAKE THAT BAT TO GAMES ANYMORE.
THAT'S NOT FAIR! DAD--
THIS ISN'T ABOUT YOUR FATHER. OR ANYONE ELSE. ZANE DID NOT HIT THAT HOME RUN TODAY. YOU DID.

THAT BAT AND THIS ZANE NONSENSE, IT'S JUST A STORY.

AND ONE I'M TIRED OF HEARING.

HE IS NOT WATCHING OVER US, ALEX.

WELL I DON'T KNOW IF IT'S ZANE OR THE FISHHOOKS OR WHATEVER... THE BAT'S GOOD LUCK.
IF DAD HAD TAKEN IT WITH HIM THAT NIGHT, HE'D STILL BE--

HE'D STILL BE DEAD, ALEX!

YOUR FATHER... HE...
THERE WAS A STORM. A STORM AND A BROKEN POWER LINE. NO ONE COULD HAVE HAD ANY CONTROL OVER THAT. DO YOU UNDERSTAND?
NO ONE.

Zane could've.
EXCUSE ME.

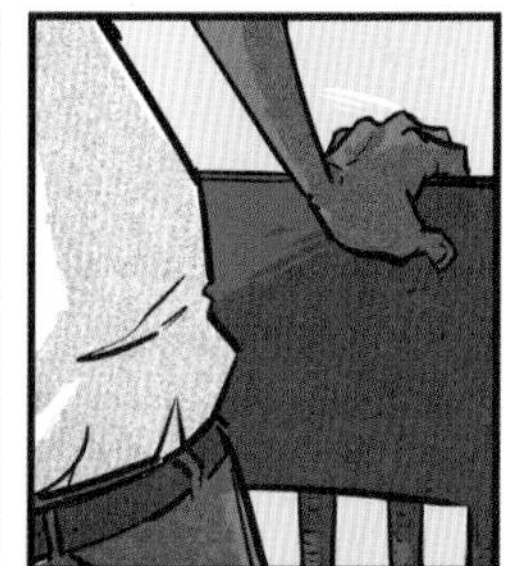

Is that so hard, you heathens?
YOU'RE WELCOME.

ALEX, I *DO* UNDERSTAND...
...THESE SUPERSTITIONS ARE IMPORTANT TO YOU. THEY REMIND YOU OF YOUR FATHER, AND I LOVE THAT.

BUT YOU HAVE TO LET GO OF THE IDEA THAT THIS STUFF CAN CONTROL YOUR FATE.
THE BAT, KNOCKING ON WOOD... THROWING OTHER PEOPLE'S SALT OVER YOUR SHOULDER?
AND NOW YOU'RE TOO SCARED TO CELEBRATE YOUR OWN BIRTHDAY BECAUSE OF A ***NUMBER.***

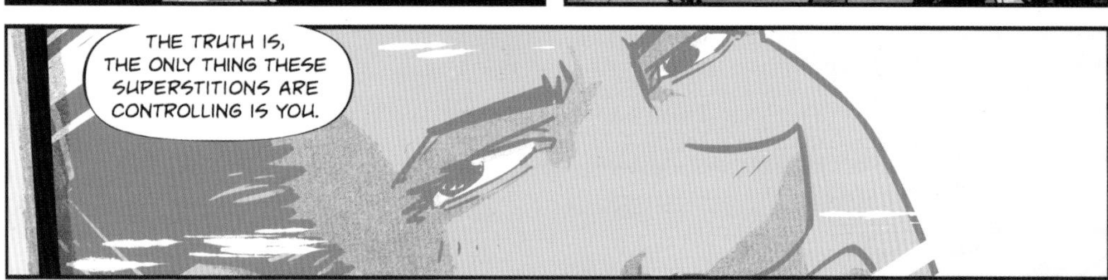
THE TRUTH IS, THE ONLY THING THESE SUPERSTITIONS ARE CONTROLLING IS YOU.

THIS IS THE FINAL WORD ON THE MATTER--YOU CAN KEEP TAKING THE BAT WITH YOU TO THE BALLPARK, BUT THE NEXT TIME YOU DON'T FOLLOW YOUR COACH'S INSTRUCTION--AND I MEAN TO THE LETTER--JUST BECAUSE YOU'D RATHER RELY ON ZANE, YOU'RE OFF THE TEAM.
BUT--

AND WE'RE GOING OUT TOMORROW NIGHT.
YOU CAN CONSIDER A FORTY-DOLLAR STEAK ON YOUR BIRTHDAY YOUR PUNISHMENT FOR ARGUING WITH ME.
FINE.
I KNOW, I'M SUCH A SHREW.

IN TWENTY MINUTES, I WANT YOU SHOWERED AND YOUR HOMEWORK STARTED.
WHATEVER...

You act like this is fun for me.
I'm trying to protect us.

"Step on a crack, break your mother's back."
A thousand times I've tip-toed across this driveway.
For your sake.

And if you ever noticed me doing it?
You'd just yell at me again.
So what do I do it for?

Fine, you want me to change my behavior?

Maybe she's right.
What'd I think was going to happen?

So stupid.

MOM!

HOSPITAL
THE DOCTORS SAY YOU'RE GONNA BE OKAY.

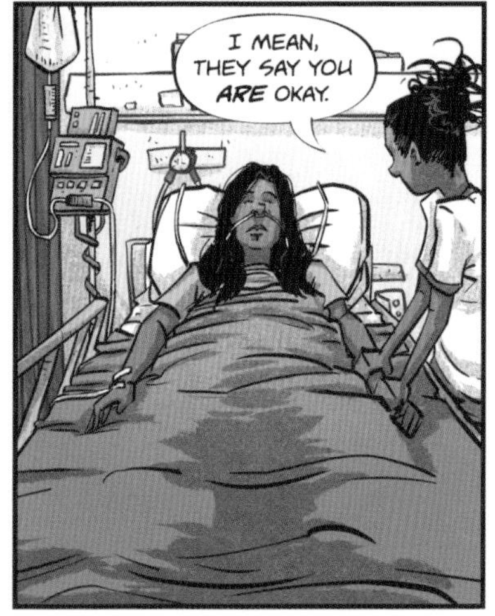
I MEAN, THEY SAY YOU *ARE* OKAY.

NO.
WHAT I MEAN IS THEY SAY YOU'RE NOT HURT. NOT THAT THEY CAN TELL.
LIKE, YOU'RE NOT REALLY INJURED, BUT YOU *ARE* PARALYZED.
IT'S LIKE YOUR BACK IS BROKEN, BUT... THEY SAID IT MIGHT BE... UH... PSYCHO... PSYCHOSOMATIC?

CAN YOU EVEN HEAR ME?
If you can, you probably won't believe what I have to say...
...this is my fault.

I was so angry at you, but I didn't think you would actually--
I don't know what I thought.
I'm so sorry.

But I'm not crazy. I know most people ignore these rules, and everything goes just fine for them. But clearly I can't.
I'm jinxed.
So I'm gonna do the same thing Zane did.
I'm gonna find Lady Luck. Somehow. I'll do whatever it takes. I swear I will. Please just hang in there until I get back.

And wish me luck.

THANKS FOR THE RIDE, COACH.
I DON'T LIKE LEAVING YOU HERE ALONE.
NO, UH, I'M NOT ALONE...

...MY GRANDFATHER'S WATCHING ME.

LOOKIE
lady luc_

Ugh!
SNAP

This is the dumbest idea I've ever had.
Zane could ride off on horseback and sleep under the stars and, you know, **quest**.
What am I supposed to do?
I'm only twelve--

Thirteen. I'm thirteen years old.
12:14

Thirteen.
Doesn't feel that different.

Maybe that's cause everything about me is already so unlucky that the number thirteen can't even make a dent.

I should call Coach. I should stay with his family.
His daughter's just a year behind me. We have choir together. I mean, I kinda hate her, but...
It could be fun in an awful sort of way.
Maybe I'll get lucky and Lady Luck will come find me. Lady Luck and Zane. Married and with, like, a thousand babies.
That'd be awesome...

What do you think, Mr. Leprechaun? Would they--

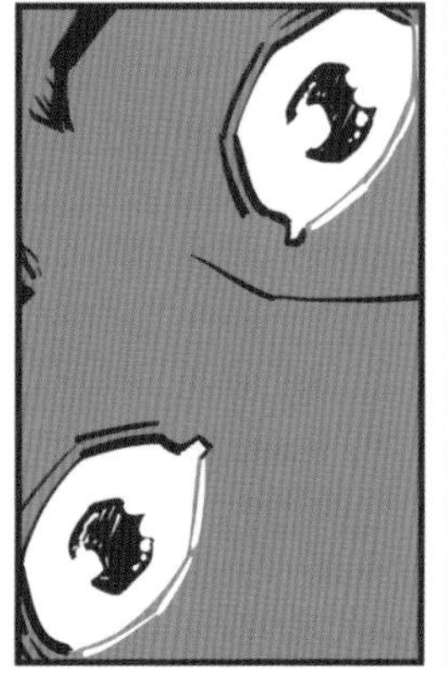

AHHHHH!

DON'T BE FRIGHTENED, LASS. THIS BLADE'S NOT FOR YOU.

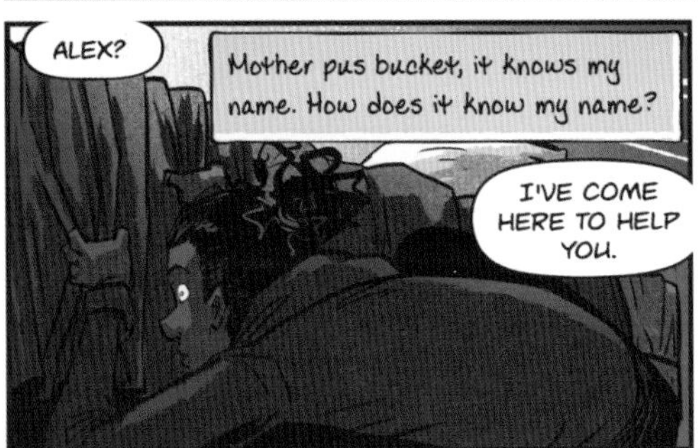

ARE YOU ONE OF HIS BABIES?!

PRETEND I DIDN'T ASK THAT.
DONE.
YOU'RE OBVIOUSLY... UH, I MEAN... DO YOU IDENTIFY AS...
LEPRECHAUN, ALEX. I'M A LEPRECHAUN.
OBVIOUSLY.
AND YOU MENTIONED MY MOM?

THERE'S AN ANTIDOTE FOR YOUR MOTHER'S CONDITION.
A RABBIT'S FOOT.

I HAVE RABBIT'S FEET. SIX OF THEM. IN THE DRAWER YOU'RE STANDING ON.

BAH! NEON COLORED KEY-CHAIN TRINKETS.

MASS PRODUCED IN SWEATSHOPS AND TRADED FOR SKEE-BALL TICKETS. TO SAVE YOUR MOM, YOU NEED THE GENUINE ARTICLE.
WELL, DID YOU BRING THE GENUINE ARTICLE WITH YOU?
COULDN'T IF I WANTED TO. YOU STEPPED ON THE CRACK. YOU HAVE TO RETRIEVE THE FOOT. MY ROLE IS TO GUIDE YOU...

...TO HAPHAVEN.

HAPHAVEN?
THE WORLD I COME FROM. THE WORLD FROM WHICH ALL YOUR SUPERSTITIONS DRAW THEIR POWER.

THE FOOT IS THERE, GUARDED BY A TERRIBLE BEAST...
THE JINX.
MISFORTUNE GIVEN PHYSICAL FORM. A TWISTED SOUL WITH NO MERCY OR KINDNESS TO BE FOUND WITHIN.
BUT DO NOT GIVE IN TO FEAR, MY SOLDIERS AND I WILL--

YES.
YES, LET'S DO IT. MAGICAL LAND. EVIL MONSTER. MYSTICAL ANTIDOTE. I'M IN.
This is so cool.

JUST LIKE THAT? REALLY?

YEAH, THIS IS GREAT. THIS KINDA THING IS, LIKE, A FAMILY TRADITION FOR ME.

WONDERFUL, THEN.

LET'S BE ON OUR WAY!

THAT'S BETTER.
BLASTED MARSHMALLOW-PEDDLIN' NONSENSE.

A GATEWAY BETWEEN WORLDS IS SET TO OPEN SOON. WE HAVE TO HURRY. ONCE IT'S OPEN, IT'LL ONLY BE ACCESSIBLE FOR A FEW MOMENTS.

I'm gonna save my mom.
Classic Mills' family adventure!
Thank you, Zane!

THERE...

...THE PRISMATIC GATEWAY!

FOLLOW IT!

WOW.
END OF THE FREAKIN' RAINBOW...

FAIR WARNING--HAPHAVEN'S A WEE BIT DIFFERENT FROM YOUR WORLD. AND IT CAN BE DANGEROUS.
I'LL BE AT YOUR SIDE, LOOKING OUT FOR YOU. BUT IF YOU GET IN A TIGHT SPOT, REMEMBER TO FALL BACK ON YOUR 'STITIONS. THE RULES YOU KNOW. OBEY THEM AT ALL TIMES, AND--

GREAT, LET'S GET MOVING.
OFF TO HAPHAVEN!
ALEX, WAIT! NO!

MOVE IT HUBBUB, YOU'RE WASTING--

WHOA!

Regret.
This sensation filling my entire being is definitely regret.

NO!
Or puke. Could be puke.

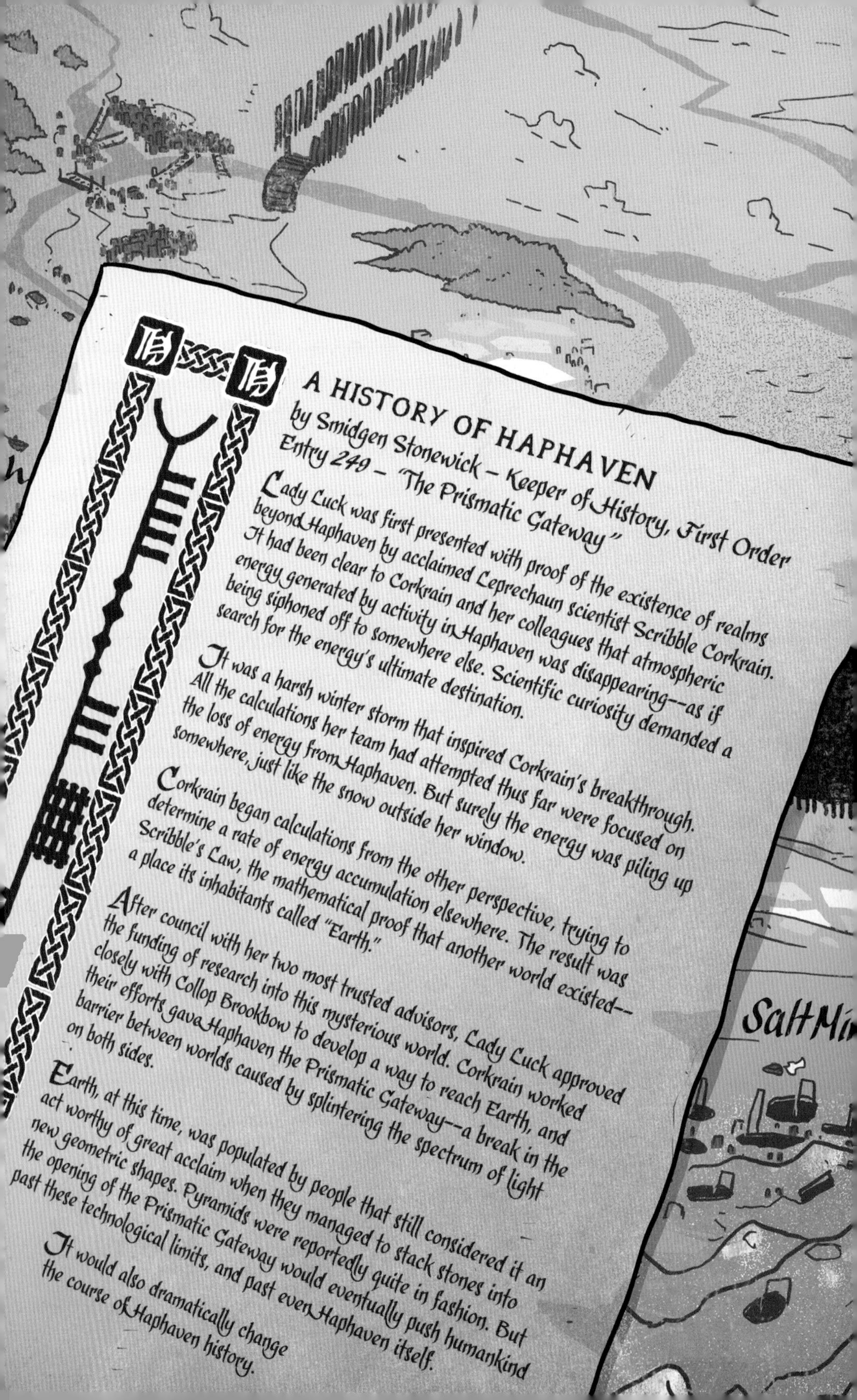
A HISTORY OF HAPHAVEN
by Smidgen Stonewick – Keeper of History, First Order
Entry 249 – "The Prismatic Gateway"
Lady Luck was first presented with proof of the existence of realms beyond Haphaven by acclaimed Leprechaun scientist Scribble Corkrain. It had been clear to Corkrain and her colleagues that atmospheric energy generated by activity in Haphaven was disappearing--as if being siphoned off to somewhere else. Scientific curiosity demanded a search for the energy's ultimate destination.
It was a harsh winter storm that inspired Corkrain's breakthrough. All the calculations her team had attempted thus far were focused on the loss of energy from Haphaven. But surely the energy was piling up somewhere, just like the snow outside her window.
Corkrain began calculations from the other perspective, trying to determine a rate of energy accumulation elsewhere. The result was Scribble's Law, the mathematical proof that another world existed--a place its inhabitants called "Earth."
After council with her two most trusted advisors, Lady Luck approved the funding of research into this mysterious world. Corkrain worked closely with Collop Brookbow to develop a way to reach Earth, and their efforts gave Haphaven the Prismatic Gateway--a break in the barrier between worlds caused by splintering the spectrum of light on both sides.
Earth, at this time, was populated by people that still considered it an act worthy of great acclaim when they managed to stack stones into new geometric shapes. Pyramids were reportedly quite in fashion. But the opening of the Prismatic Gateway would eventually push humankind past these technological limits, and past even Haphaven itself.
It would also dramatically change the course of Haphaven history.

Chapter 2

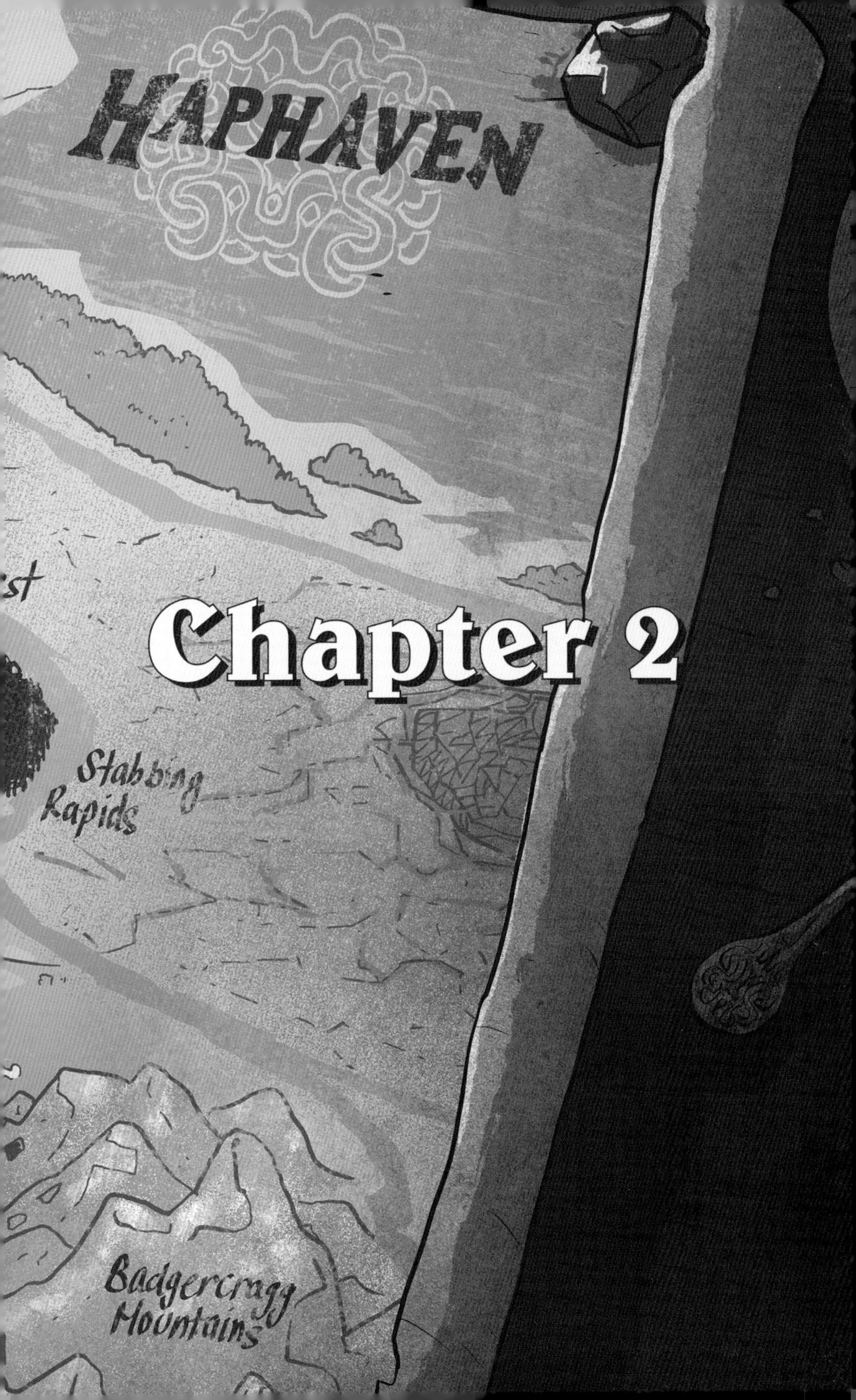

CRAACK

AHHHHH!

Salt.
PTTU--
Strange magic land, no bat, no warrior leprechaun guide.
And I just spilled ALL of the salt.
--PFFFT...
Alex's luck strikes again.

Maybe at least these guys can point me in the right direction.
HEY... I'M SORRY...
They look angry.
LISTEN... I CAN HELP YOU CLEAN THIS--

OW!

HEY, HEY, HOLD ON! WAIT A MINUTE!
I officially hate Leprechauns.

Shoot...
Can't see a flippin' thing with those miners' lights in my face. How do I fight back if I can't see?
LISTEN, THIS WAS AN ACCIDENT. YOU'RE OBVIOUSLY ALL VERY, UH, DEDICATED WORKERS. MAYBE YOU'VE GOT SOME UNION, UH, RULES ABOUT... PLEASE, I DIDN'T MEAN TO SPILL YOUR...
Duh, Alex. You spilled salt!
Salt that's big and coarse... probably like hail stones to them...
This is what Hubbub was just talking about. I think. I should have listened more.
I can't face these little jerks without the light blinding me...
...but if I make it rain...
GAH!
ARGH!
BAH!

LAST TIME THE BARREL BROKE IT TOOK SEVEN LADS OUTTA CLOVERHEAD TO DO IT.

AND THEY ONLY SPILLED ABOUT HALF THIS MUCH. THAT'S USING EXPLOSIVES, MIND YOU.

COURSE, THEY WEREN'T QUITE AS GARGANTUAN AS YOU ARE.

YOU FROM CLOVERHEAD?

I'M REALLY SORRY.

SHE'S GETTIN' AWAY, PENNY!
YES, I CAN SEE THAT.

Wait a second.
YOUR NAME'S PENNY?

PENWYN COPPERLONG. BUT FOLKS CALL ME PENNY. WHAT OF IT?

SWEET SODIUM, WHAT ARE YOU DOING?

YOU'RE PUTTIN' ME BEHIND SCHEDULE!
Leprechauns have no chill.
Maybe it's because they're so small.
Like Chihuahuas.

HEY! I WAS JUST TRYING TO TALK TO YOU!

LISTEN TO ME! I NEED YOUR HELP.
WITH WHAT?
SAVING MY MOTHER. SHE'S HURT, AND--
I'VE GOT A LOT OF SKILLS, LASS, BUT "DOCTOR" AIN'T AMONG THEM.

IT'S NOT LIKE THAT.

I HAVE TO RETRIEVE A CHARM FROM THE JINX--
--AND YOU'RE A PENNY!
"FIND A PENNY, PICK IT UP, ALL DAY LONG YOU'LL HAVE GOOD LUCK."
THE JINX?! YOU MEAN TO CART ME OFF ON SOME SUICIDE MISSION AGAINST *THE JINX*?
ARE YOU GONE IN THE HEAD?
SORRY, PENNY. YOU DON'T GET A SAY IN THIS.
I already lost my bat. I can't go questing with nothing.
An angry good luck charm is better than none at all.

HELP!
HI.
HEEELLLPPPP!
SORRY TO BOTHER YOU. I'M LOOKING FOR--
YOU HAVE TO HELP ME! SEND WORD TO SEAMRÓG CASTLE! HAVE 'EM SEND THE ROYAL GUARD!
THAT WOULD BE GREAT! I'M ACTUALLY WORKING WITH THE ROYAL GUARD.
I THINK.
FINALLY...
HUH
HUH

WHUH WHUH WHUH

...THE AUTHORITIES!

MY BAT!

ALEX, THANK HEAVEN WE FOUND YOU. I WORRIED THAT RAINBOW MIGHT'VE SPIT YOU HALFWAY TO RAVENGLEN.

SALT MINE, ACTUALLY.
AH. DID THEY HURT YOU?
I'M OKAY. MOSTLY. THREW SALT AT 'EM. OVER THE SHOULDER, SO THEIR LIGHTS DIDN'T BLIND ME.
FOLLOWED THE 'STITIONS. WELL DONE, LASS.

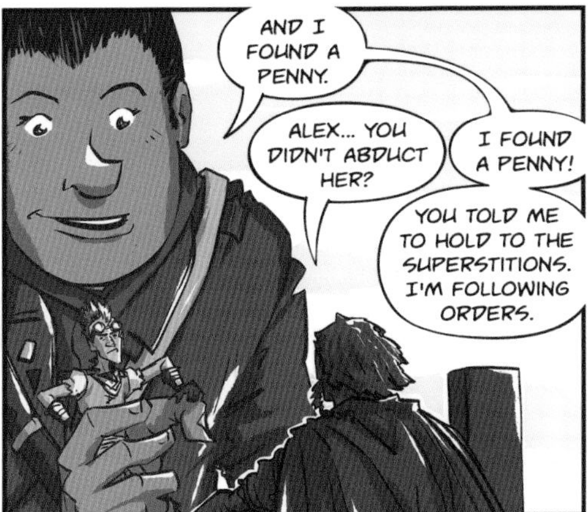

AND I FOUND A PENNY.
ALEX... YOU DIDN'T ABDUCT HER?
I FOUND A PENNY!
YOU TOLD ME TO HOLD TO THE SUPERSTITIONS. I'M FOLLOWING ORDERS.

MA'AM, YOU HAVE MY SINCEREST APOLOGIES.
WE'RE CHARGED WITH TAKING THE LASS HERE ON A MISSION.
I TRIED TO TELL YOU...

ALL RIGHT, MS...?
COPPERLONG. PENWYN COPPERLONG.
MS. COPPERLONG, I'LL HAVE A DETAIL ESCORT YOU BACK TO THE MINE AND--
I DON'T KNOW ABOUT THAT. THOUGHT THE LASS WAS A MONSTER HERSELF, BUT IF SHE'S ALIGNED WITH THE ROYAL GUARD...
YOU REALLY SENDIN' THIS YOUNG LADY AGAINST THE JINX?

WE ARE. LASS NEEDS SOMETHING IT'S GOT. SOMETHING ONLY SHE CAN RETRIEVE.
I SEE...
WELL, TRUTH OF IT IS, SHE'S RIGHT ABOUT PICKING ME UP.

I KNEW IT!

I HAVEN'T ALWAYS BEEN A MINE FOREMAN. I JOIN UP AT FARMS, FACTORIES... ANYPLACE THAT'S IN A BAD WAY. I COME IN, TAKE CONTROL. CRACK THE WHIP. I FIX THINGS.
YOU GET ME ON YOUR TEAM, AND I TURN YOUR FORTUNE AROUND.
THAT'S MY PLACE IN THE WORLD.

I DON'T USUALLY LIKE THE FOLKS I WORK FOR VERY MUCH.
THEY TEND TO BE SLOPPY, DISORGANIZED, IMPULSIVE, AND IN OVER THEIR HEADS.
BUT I GUESS IF THEY WERE THE KINDA FOLK I LIKED, THEN THEY PROBABLY WOULDN'T NEED MY HELP IN THE FIRST PLACE.

I HAVE TO SAY, SOMETHING ABOUT THIS MAKES ME THINK YOU'RE ALL IN OVER YOUR HEADS.
AND I PROBABLY LIKE YOU LESS THAN ANYONE I'VE EVER MET, RAINBOW GIRL.

BESIDES, THE MINE'S IN SHAMBLES NOW. NOT MUCH I CAN DO THERE WHILE THEY REBUILD.
SO YOU HAVE TO COME WITH ME. JUST UNTIL I GET THIS RABBIT'S FOOT?

...
RIGHT, LET'S GO.
LORD HELP ME.

'FRAID I CAN'T ALLOW THIS. ABSOLUTELY NOT.
NO, SHE COMES.
ALL DUE RESPECT, ALEX, WE HAVE A STRATEGY AND MS. COPPERLONG HERE ISN'T PART OF IT.
YOUR MOTHER'S AT STAKE.

THAT'S WHY SHE'S COMING. I'M DOING EVERYTHING BY THE SUPERSTITION BOOK. OBEY THE RULES, TO THE LETTER. LIKE YOU TOLD ME TO. IF I'M FIGHTING THIS JINX THING, THEN I'LL NEED ALL THE HELP I CAN GET.
THERE'S NO RULE THAT SAYS I NEED TO CARRY A HUBBUB AT MY SIDE.
BUT I FOUND A PENNY. AND I'VE PICKED IT UP.
SO WE'RE MOVING OUT.
YOU CAN TAG ALONG IF YOU WANT.

FINE. YOUR CALL.
DON'T BLAME ME WHEN WE ALL END UP MINCE PIES FOR THE JINX.

THERE IT IS...

...SLUGWOOD FOREST.

I REMEMBER MY LAST TIME GOING UP AGAINST THE JINX.

CAUGHT THE BEAST IN THE MIDDLE OF A HUNT. SAW IT RIP A BOAR IN TWO WITH ITS BARE HANDS.

THE THING ABOUT THE JINX THAT ALWAYS GIVES ME A SHIVER...
THE SMELL.
TOK
ITS CLOTHES, ALWAYS WET. MILDEWY AND... BLECCCH.

I HEAR ITS SKIN'S AS DISEASED AS A STAGNANT BOG.

LET IT TOUCH YOU, AND WITHIN A DAY YOU'LL BE FIGHTING TO KEEP YOUR INSIDES INSIDE.

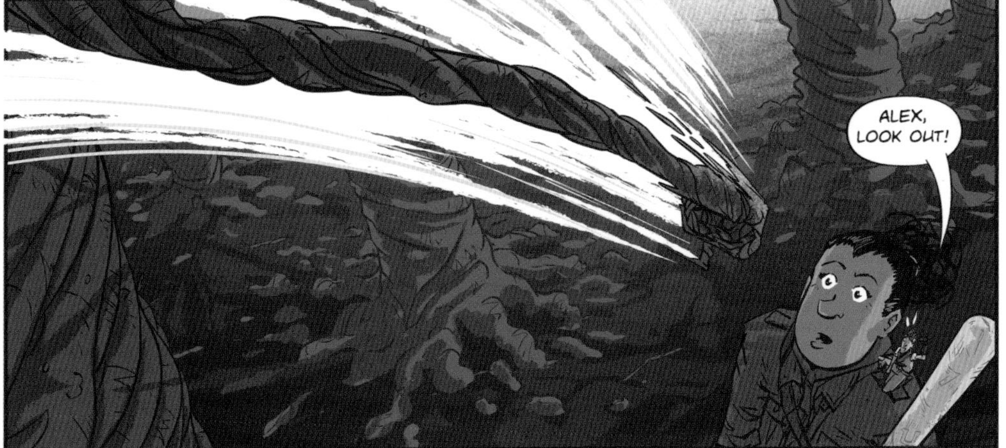
ALEX, LOOK OUT!

I DON'T UNDERSTAND, I HIT THE TREE. WHY DIDN'T YOU TELL ME THEY WERE GONNA HIT BACK?
YOU KNOCKED ON ONE. THEY DON'T HIT BACK, THEY HIT FIRST. BUT ONLY IF YOU LET 'EM. SLUGWOOD RESPECTS A PREEMPTIVE STRIKE. EVERY TREE YOU PASS.

BUT YOU WEREN'T KNOCKING ON THEM.
WELL THEY CAN'T REACH US, CAN THEY?
LET'S KEEP MOVIN'.

"They can't reach us."
THIS WORLD OF YOURS--
CRACK
--IS A LITTLE RIDICULOUS. DON'T YOU THINK?

RIDICULOUS IS RELATIVE. TO US, THIS IS HOME.
YOU WANT TO SURVIVE IT, RESPECT IT.

I'M SORRY, WAS I NOT--
CRACK
--PROPERLY RESPECTING YOUR MURDEROUS TREES?

SKREEEEEEEEEEEEEEEE
WHAT WAS THAT? THE JINX?
IMPS. I WAS HOPING WE'D BE IN AND OUT BEFORE THEY STARTED HUNTING FOR THE DAY, BUT THAT SALT MINE DETOUR SET US BACK.
IMPS?
PREDATORS THAT LIVE IN SLUGWOOD.
MISCHIEVOUS TROUBLEMAKERS ON THEIR BEST DAY, BLOODTHIRSTY ON THEIR WORST.
YOU... UH... YOU THINK THIS IS ONE OF THEIR BEST DAYS?

NOPE.

LUCK BE WITH YOUR BLADES!
ALEX, DUCK!

Stupid.

LISTEN UP, RAINBOW GIRL.
YOU WANTED A GOOD LUCK CHARM, SO HERE'S WHERE YOU GET ONE.
THIS ISN'T YOUR FIGHT.

BUT HUBBUB'S--
--NOT YOUR FRIEND.
HE'S A SOLDIER WHO BROUGHT YOU HERE TO FIGHT A BATTLE HE CAN'T. WHICH MEANS HE'S NO HELP TO YOU.
FIND THE JINX, FIND THE FOOT. THAT'S YOUR ONLY CONCERN.
BUT--
YOU WANT THE FOOT? IT'S WITH THE JINX, AT THE CENTER OF SLUGWOOD.
STAND UP, GRAB YOUR BAT, AND RUN.

YOU PICKED ME UP, THIS IS WHAT YOU GET. YOU DON'T WANT THE ADVICE? I'M HAPPY TO WALK.
AIN'T MY MOTHER ON THE LINE.

NO... YOU'RE RIGHT.

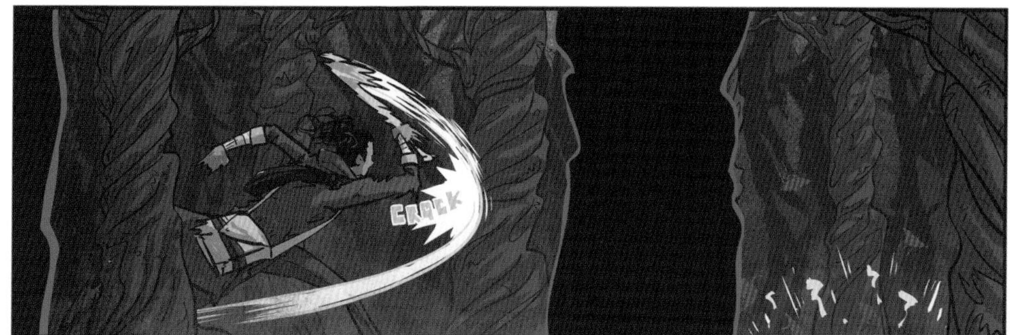
CRACK

ALEX, NO! WAIT!
BLOODY COPPERLONG.

CRACK

CRACK

CRACK
CRACK

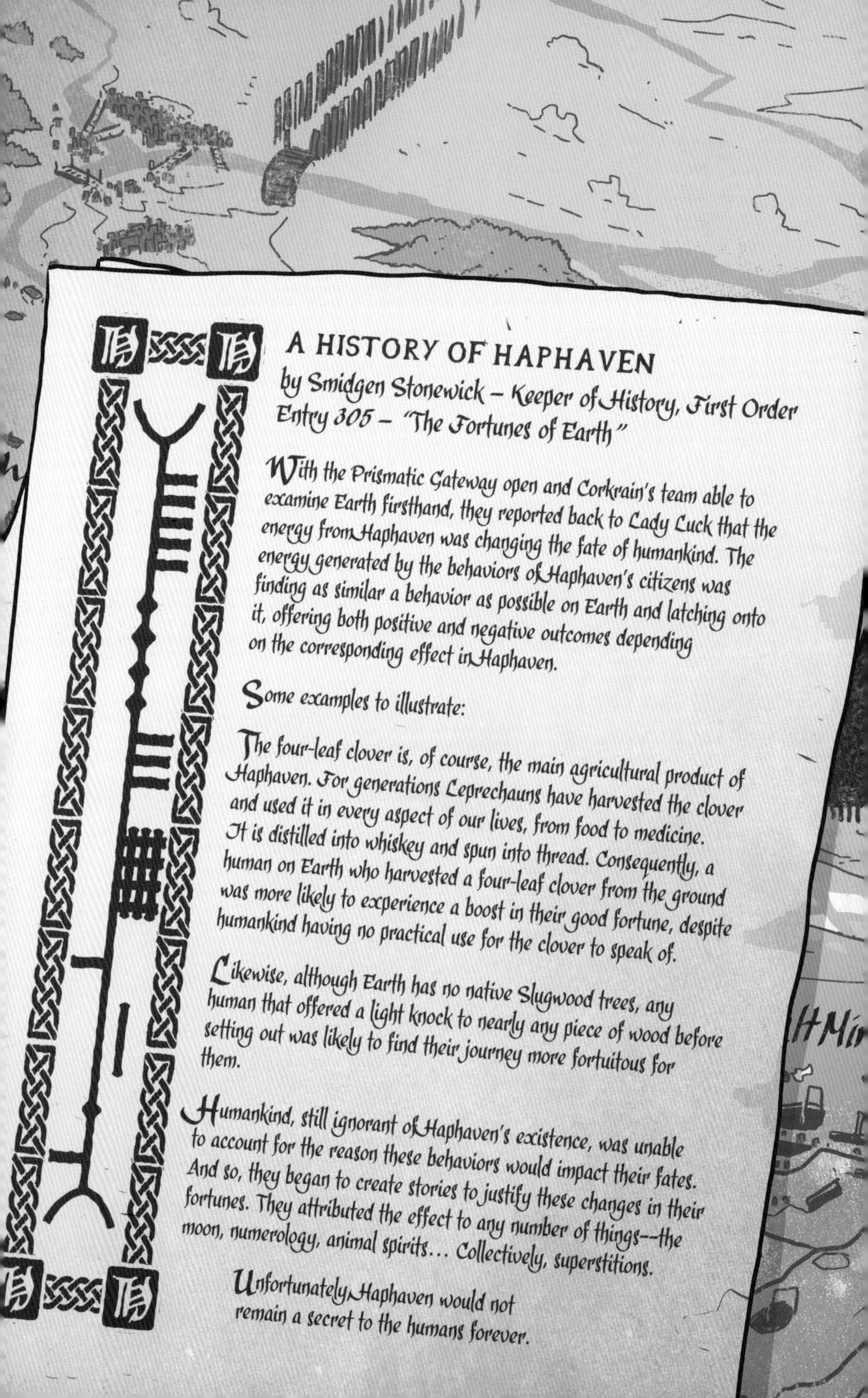

A HISTORY OF HAPHAVEN

by Smidgen Stonewick – Keeper of History, First Order
Entry 305 – "The Fortunes of Earth"

With the Prismatic Gateway open and Corkrain's team able to examine Earth firsthand, they reported back to Lady Luck that the energy from Haphaven was changing the fate of humankind. The energy generated by the behaviors of Haphaven's citizens was finding as similar a behavior as possible on Earth and latching onto it, offering both positive and negative outcomes depending on the corresponding effect in Haphaven.

Some examples to illustrate:

The four-leaf clover is, of course, the main agricultural product of Haphaven. For generations Leprechauns have harvested the clover and used it in every aspect of our lives, from food to medicine. It is distilled into whiskey and spun into thread. Consequently, a human on Earth who harvested a four-leaf clover from the ground was more likely to experience a boost in their good fortune, despite humankind having no practical use for the clover to speak of.

Likewise, although Earth has no native Slugwood trees, any human that offered a light knock to nearly any piece of wood before setting out was likely to find their journey more fortuitous for them.

Humankind, still ignorant of Haphaven's existence, was unable to account for the reason these behaviors would impact their fates. And so, they began to create stories to justify these changes in their fortunes. They attributed the effect to any number of things--the moon, numerology, animal spirits... Collectively, superstitions.

Unfortunately Haphaven would not remain a secret to the humans forever.

Chapter 3

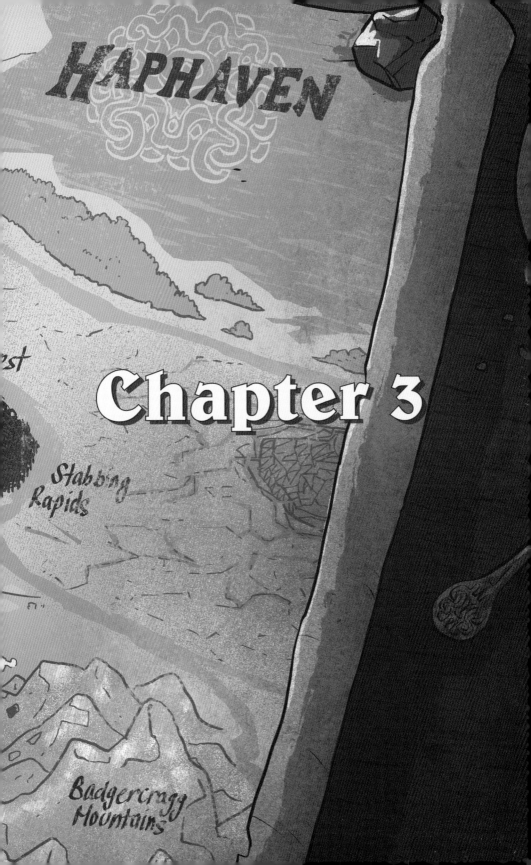

HELLO?
PENNY, THIS WAS MAYBE NOT THE BEST PLAN. I THINK WE SHOULD GO BACK TO--

TAKE THINGS SLOW, KEEP YOUR HEAD ABOUT YOU.
DON'T WORRY, I'M WITH YOU.
GREAT. BETWEEN YOU AND ME WE'VE GOT A COMBINED HEIGHT OF FIVE FEET, SIX INCHES.
MISFORTUNE MONSTERS BEWARE...

Oh boy.

This is gonna suck.

HELLO?

Just keep thinking about Mom.

YOU
LOST, LITTLE
GIRL?

I'M JUST HERE FOR THE RABBIT'S FOOT. PLEASE--

I DON'T CARE IF YOU WANT A FOOT, AN EAR, OR A LITTLE COTTONTAIL, ALL YOU'RE GONNA END UP GETTIN' IS A WORLD OF HURT!

WHAT? NO, I JUST CAME FOR THE FOOT.
IT'S LIKE A TALISMAN, IT'S PROBABLY ON A CHAIN--

ON A CHAIN? WHAT EXACTLY DO YOU THINK--

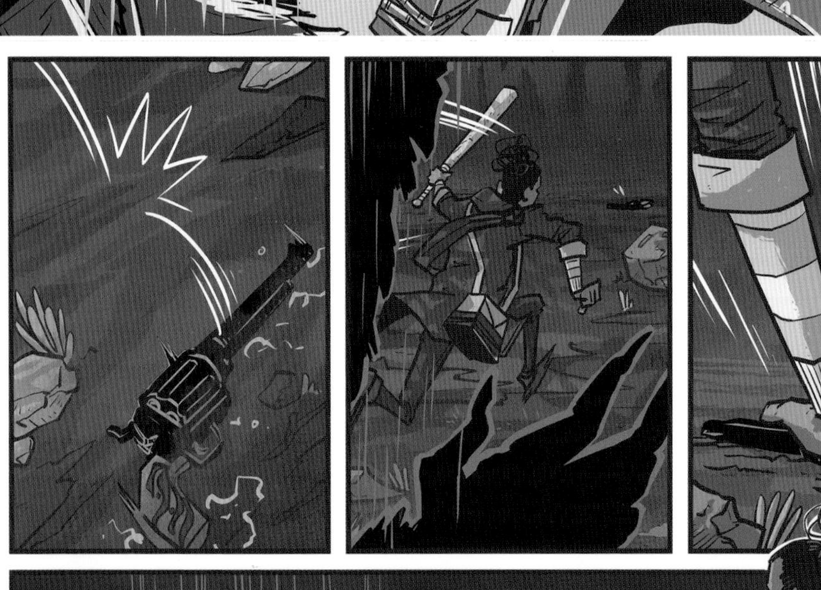

DRAW.

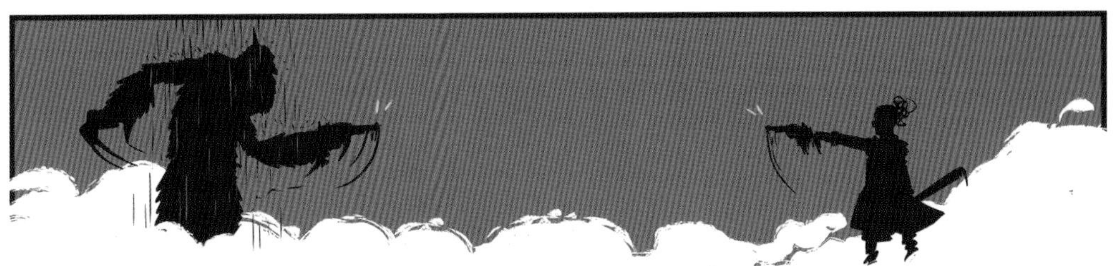

Whoa. I wasn't bluffing.

What the--

JINXED SIX SHOOTER, KID.
AMMO'S UNLIMITED, BUT YOU NEVER KNOW WHAT'S GONNA COME TUMBLIN' OUT OF THE BARREL.

YOU GOT HEART. AND A NICE BUNCH OF LUCKY CHARMS CARVED INTO THIS BAT ALREADY.
BUT I NEED THE FOOT.
MY MOM'S HURT AND IT'S THE ONLY THING THAT CAN HEAL HER.

AND THAT'S THE ONLY EXPLANATION FOR YOU TREKKING ALL THE WAY OUT HERE? JUST LOOKING TO FIND SOME SORTA MATRIARCHAL SNAKE OIL?

THE FOOT'S THE ONLY THING THAT WILL SAVE HER. THAT'S ALL I WANT.

YEAH, OKAY.
OKAY?
I'LL TAKE YOU TO THIS FOOT YOU'RE LOOKIN' FOR.

BUT I GOTTA WARN YA, BE PREPARED FOR DISAPPOINTMENT.

AFTER YOU.

SO... DID YOU BUILD THAT, UH, GHOST TOWN UP THERE?

FOUND IT LIKE THAT.

USED TO BE MORE TYPES IN HAPHAVEN THAN JUST LEPRECHAUNS.

BUT THAT WAS LONG BEFORE I GOT HERE.

SO, WAIT, WHERE DO JINXES COME FROM? DID YOU TRAVEL THROUGH THE, UH, PRISMATIC RAINBOW THINGY, TOO?

SHUT UP AND KEEP WALKING.

SORRY, I JUST... YOU KNOW... I'M NERVOUS AND NEW TO THE WHOLE MAGICAL REALM TRAVEL SCENE.
SO MANY QUESTIONS.
LIKE, WITH THAT CLOUD, DO YOU EXPERIENCE, LIKE, PERSONAL RAINBOWS? IS THAT A--
I SAID QUIET.

I'LL BE QUIET.

YOU KNOW, I WAS THINKING...

...WHAT I NEED DOWN HERE IS SOME MUSIC. I **MISS** MUSIC.
YOU THINK YOU COULD SWING BRINGING ME A DRUM OR--
WAIT, WHAT IS THIS?

YOU'RE BRINGING ME VISITORS NOW?

YOU FINALLY TAKE ONE TOO MANY LIGHTNING BOLTS TO THE CRANIUM?
WHAT COULD POSSIBLY BE RUNNING THROUGH THAT DAMP, MOLDY SKULL OF YOURS THAT YOU THOUGHT BRINGING SOMEONE DOWN HERE WAS A GOOD IDEA?
WHO EVEN IS THIS?
GIRL'S HERE FOR YOUR FOOT. S'GONNA SAVE HER MOMMA.
HOW'S MY FOOT GONNA SAVE HER MOMMA?

I'M JUST AS CURIOUS ABOUT THAT AS YOU ARE.
WAIT... AREN'T YOU... IS THAT... ARE YOU WEARING A COAT?
OTTER HIDE. KEEPS THE RAIN OFF. SKINNED 'EM MYSELF...

...WITH THIS.
GO AHEAD, GIRL. MAKE IT "JUST A FOOT."
JUST SO EVERYONE'S CLEAR, I'M NOT AN OTTER!

DON'T GET YOUR EARS IN A KNOT, SHE AIN'T GONNA DO IT.
HOW DO YOU KNOW?
WHAT, BECAUSE SHE'S HUMAN? YOU'VE NEVER KNOWN A HUMAN TO DO SOMETHING TERRIBLE?
DID YOU EVEN SEARCH HER FIRST?

AIN'T NO NEED TO SEARCH HER. LOOK AT HER, SHE'S JUST A LITTLE--
IN HER POCKET. SOMETHING JUST MOVED IN HER POCKET!

TARNATION...
...WE GOT OURSELVES A LEPRECHAUN.

WHOA!
KEEP LOOKING! SHE COULD HAVE THE ENTIRE ROYAL GUARD IN THAT COAT.

YOU'VE GOT IT WRONG.
THE LASS WASN'T TRYING TO AMBUSH YOU.
YOU STAY QUIET, WE'LL FIGURE THIS OUT.

WHAT'S THIS?

YOU LYIN' LITTLE SNEAK.
WHAT'CHA GOT?

SECRET MESSAGE?
ORDERS FROM THE THRONE.
HAS TO BE.

WHAT'RE YOU PLAYIN' AT, GIRL? SMUGGLING LEPRECHAUNS IN YOUR POCKET, SECRET DISPATCHES...
I HAVE NO IDEA WHAT THAT IS, I SWEAR!
I DIDN'T KNOW IT WAS IN MY JACKET! I PROMISE!
PLEASE BELIEVE ME.
PLEASE.

OKAY, WHY DON'T *YOU* TRY EXPLAINING THINGS? YOU DON'T LOOK LIKE A SOLDIER...
JUST A FRIEND OF THE LASS. HELPING HER FIND A CURE FOR HER MOTHER, LIKE SHE SAYS. WE HEARD A RABBIT'S FOOT WOULD DO THE TRICK.

SO YOU WERE OUT SEARCHING FOR MY DISMEMBERED BODY PARTS? AND THAT WAS OKAY WITH YOU?
I MEAN, I ASSUME YOU KNOW WHO I AM.

RUMORS OUT THERE SAY YOU'D BEEN DEAD A LONG TIME. FIGURED THE JINX HAD SOMETHING TO DO WITH IT.
SEEMED REASONABLE THAT HE'D HAVE YOUR FOOT.
THAT DOES MAKE AN ODD SORT OF SENSE, ACTUALLY.

Stay cool. For Mom. Get the bunny back to Hubbub and everything will be fine. Just obey the rules.

There are no rules for this!
Talking rabbits? Middle Earth Yosemite Sam? This is insane!
Okay, screw it...

I'M SORRY, LISTEN, I DIDN'T KNOW I WAS COMING AFTER AN ENTIRE RABBIT.
THIS HAS ALL BEEN A BIG MISUNDERSTANDING.

WHOA!

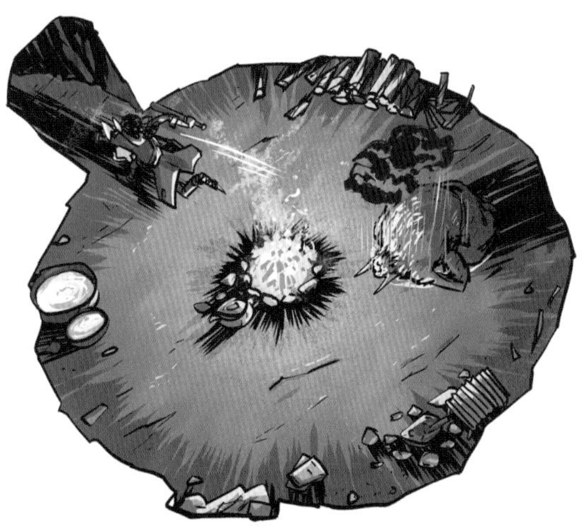

STUPID GIRL.

ALEX, THERE YOU ARE!

WITH THE ***WHOLE*** RABBIT?

WHERE'S THE--

BLOODY COPPERLONG.

BLAM

HA!
I don't know why he's even trying, those guns are use--

I wanna go home.

WHAT'RE YOU DOING, LOVE?

I DON'T KNOW.
JUST WATCH THE RABBIT. MAKE SURE HE DOESN'T TAKE OFF. I'M GONNA TRY AND DRAW THE JINX AWAY.
IF ANYTHING HAPPENS TO ME, GET THAT RABBIT TO HUBBUB. FOR MY MOM.

BLAM
BLAM
BLAM

BLAM
BLAM

BLAM

Yes!

WELL DONE, LASS!

HUBBUB. GOOD TO SEE YOU AGAIN.
"HELLO, RABBIT, HOW ARE YOU?"
I SEE YOU'RE STILL IN THE ROYAL GUARD. YOU REALLY DO TAKE THAT OATH TO THE THRONE SERIOUSLY.
"WELL, YOU KNOW ME, RABBIT. DUTY AND HONOR ABOVE ALL ELSE. EVEN WHEN IT MEANS SERVING A SLIMEBALL."
YEAH, CLASSIC HUBBUB.

Now THAT is a home run.
Thank you--

Wait a second...

CHAIN THE JINX. AND TAKE THAT BLOODY RAINCOAT OFF OF HIM. HE'S NOT EARNED A RESPITE FROM HIS CURSE.
HOW'S YOUR SISTER? SHE EVER ASK ABOUT ME?
"OH, RABBIT, YOU'RE ALL SHE--"
AND GAG THE RABBIT!

THIS... THIS IS ZANE. WHY DIDN'T YOU TELL ME?
FORGET ABOUT THE FOOT FOR A SECOND!
ALEX, WE NEED YOU TO TAKE THE FOOT--

THE FOOT IS THE MISSION! THAT'S WHAT WE'RE HERE FOR.
YOU'VE GOT FAMILY TO WORRY ABOUT, LASS.

I KNOW I DO! THAT'S WHAT I'M TALKING ABOUT! YOU SAID I WAS COMING HERE TO SAVE MY MOM **AND** ZANE.
I TOLD YOU ZANE'S FATE WAS TIED TO THE MISSION. AND IT WAS.
I WANT TO TALK TO LADY LUCK.
I'M NOT CUTTING ANYTHING OR FIGHTING ANYTHING OR TALKING TO ANYONE ELSE UNTIL I TALK TO HER.

SORRY IF I WASN'T CLEAR WITH YOU. LADY LUCK PASSED ON. MORE THAN A CENTURY AGO...

...WHEN THE JINX KILLED HER.

THEN... JUST...
TAKE ME TO WHOEVER'S IN CHARGE!
YOU HEARD HER, MATES. WE'RE SEAMRÓG BOUND.

MY DAD USED TO TELL ME STORIES ABOUT A MAN, HIS GAMBLING, AND HIS LUCKY CHARM...

...THE FISHHOOKS. THEY SAY HIS LUCKY CARDS FAILED HIM, AND HIS FAMILY KICKED HIM OUT.
SO HE WENT OFF IN SEARCH OF LADY LUCK.
DID YOU DO WHAT HUBBUB SAID?
DID YOU FIND HER?
DID YOU KILL HER?

I OUGHT TO LOCK YOU IN THE CARGO HOLD WITH THE RABBIT, COPPERLONG.

I NEED TO KNOW THAT WHEN WE GET TO SEAMRÓG YOU'LL STAY IN LINE.
THE KING... WELL, HE CAN BE LESS UNDERSTANDING THAN I AM.

I'VE DONE MORE THAN MY SHARE OF TIME ON CREWS WORKING IN AND AROUND SEAMRÓG.
I'M FAMILIAR WITH THE NECESSARY DECORUM.
BUT THE GIRL'S PICKED UP PENWYN COPPERLONG. SHE'S GOING TO GET THE BEST I CAN OFFER HER.
I'LL HAVE TO WEIGH THAT DUTY AGAINST WHAT MAKES THE KING HAPPY.
WEIGH IT WELL AND WEIGH IT QUICK, WE'RE HERE.

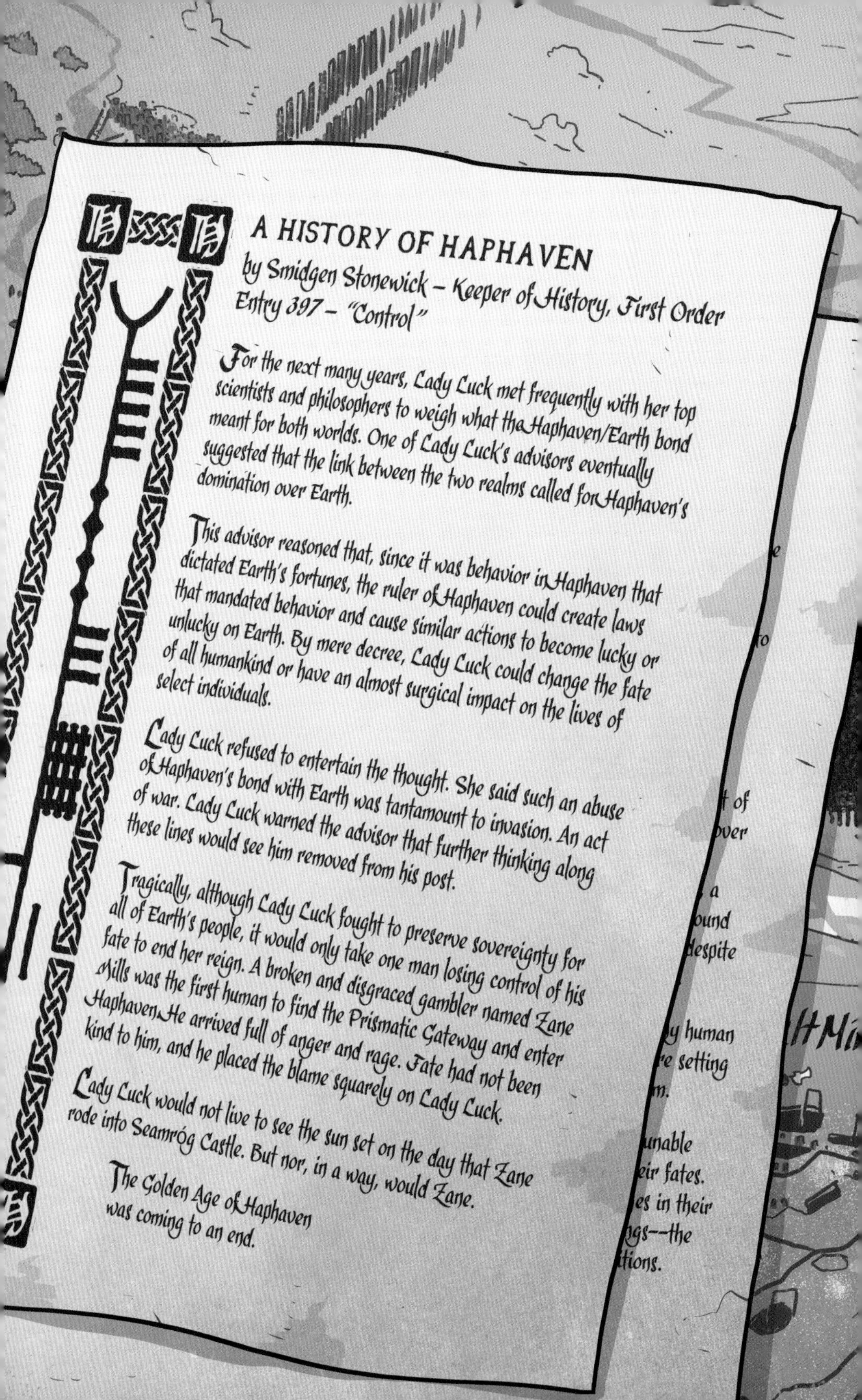

A HISTORY OF HAPHAVEN

by Smidgen Stonewick – Keeper of History, First Order

Entry 397 – "Control"

For the next many years, Lady Luck met frequently with her top scientists and philosophers to weigh what the Haphaven/Earth bond meant for both worlds. One of Lady Luck's advisors eventually suggested that the link between the two realms called for Haphaven's domination over Earth.

This advisor reasoned that, since it was behavior in Haphaven that dictated Earth's fortunes, the ruler of Haphaven could create laws that mandated behavior and cause similar actions to become lucky or unlucky on Earth. By mere decree, Lady Luck could change the fate of all humankind or have an almost surgical impact on the lives of select individuals.

Lady Luck refused to entertain the thought. She said such an abuse of Haphaven's bond with Earth was tantamount to invasion. An act of war. Lady Luck warned the advisor that further thinking along these lines would see him removed from his post.

Tragically, although Lady Luck fought to preserve sovereignty for all of Earth's people, it would only take one man losing control of his fate to end her reign. A broken and disgraced gambler named Zane Mills was the first human to find the Prismatic Gateway and enter Haphaven. He arrived full of anger and rage. Fate had not been kind to him, and he placed the blame squarely on Lady Luck.

Lady Luck would not live to see the sun set on the day that Zane rode into Seamróg Castle. But nor, in a way, would Zane.

The Golden Age of Haphaven was coming to an end.

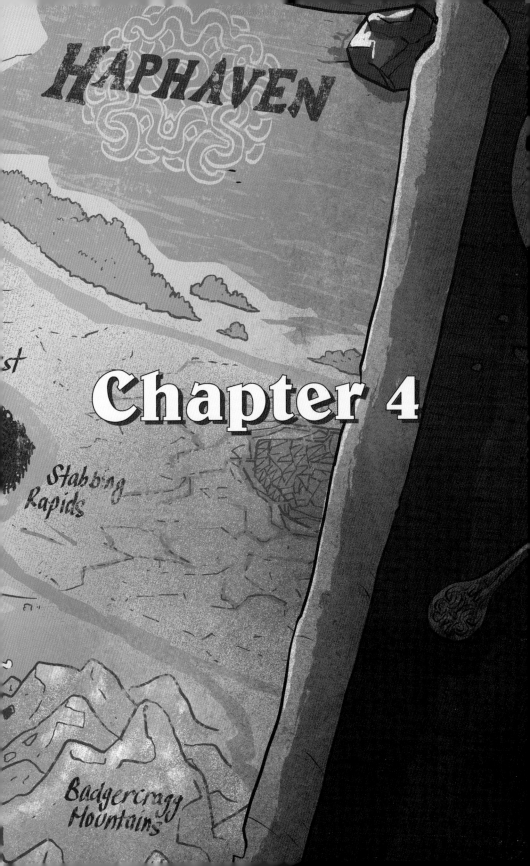

Chapter 4

HAPHAVEN
st
Stabbing Rapids
Badgercragg Mountains

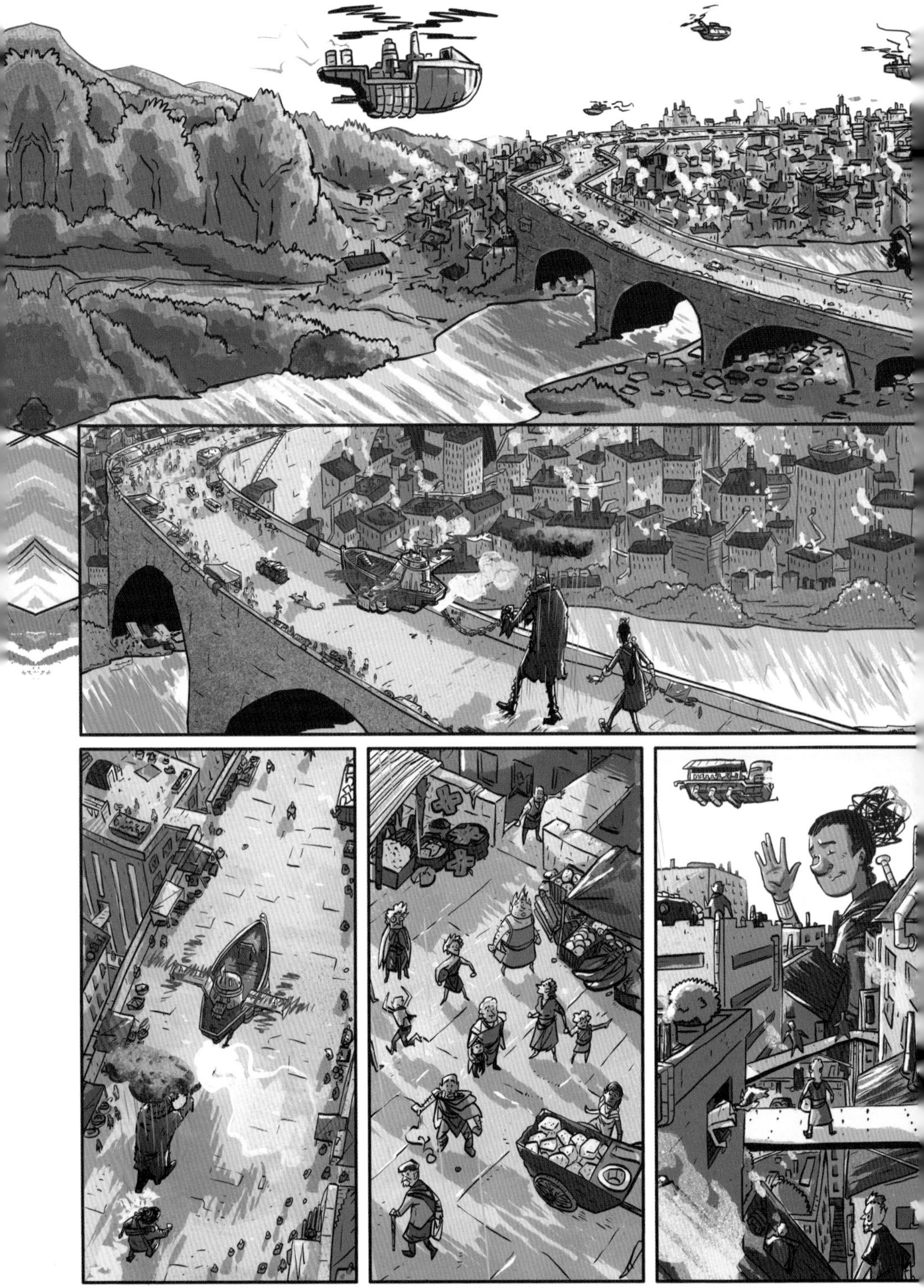

ALEX! IT IS SO TREMENDOUS TO FINALLY MEET YOU.
PLEASE, COME IN.

No...
OH, ALEX... DEAR GIRL. DEEP BREATHS. RELAX.
...it can't be.

I'M SURE YOU'VE REALIZED BY NOW THAT SOME OF YOUR SUPERSTITIONS HAVE BEEN... LET'S SAY "LOST IN TRANSLATION."
YES, IT *IS* BAD LUCK TO CROSS A BLACK CAT.
BUT THAT DOESN'T MEAN TO "STUMBLE UPON" OR "PASS BY."
RATHER "CROSS" AS IN "TO MAKE ANGRY."
"TO TRY HIS PATIENCE."
"TO TICK HIM THE HECK OFF."
IS THAT CLEARER?
NOTHING'S CLEAR ANYMORE.
I JUST WANT MY MOM TO BE OKAY. I DON'T UNDERSTAND... HOW WILL THE FOOT HELP HER?
IS IT... BECAUSE OF THE JINX? BECAUSE OF WHO HE IS?
WHO *I* AM?

YES.
I'M AFRAID SO.
OVER A HUNDRED YEARS AGO LADY LUCK SAT UPON THIS THRONE. I SAT TO HER RIGHT, THE RABBIT TO HER LEFT. WE WERE HER ADVISORS. IT WAS A GOLDEN AGE FOR HAPHAVEN. ALL WAS IN BALANCE.
UNTIL A STRANGER ARRIVED--
TO FIND OUT WHY HIS FISHHOOKS FAILED HIM?
OH NO. HE WASN'T SEEKING ANSWERS. HE SOUGHT REVENGE.
ALMOST AS SOON AS HE ENTERED THE THRONE ROOM, HE DREW A KNIFE...
...AND LUNGED FOR LADY LUCK.
THERE WAS NOTHING I COULD DO TO STOP HIM.
I TAKE SOME SMALL COMFORT IN THAT HER DEATH WAS QUICK. SHE THANKFULLY DIDN'T SUFFER.
AND AS ZANE LOOKED AT HER LIFELESS BODY, HIS OWN FORM BEGAN TO CHANGE. THE ACT OF KILLING LADY LUCK HAD CURSED HIM. ON THE DAY SHE DIED, THE JINX WAS BORN.

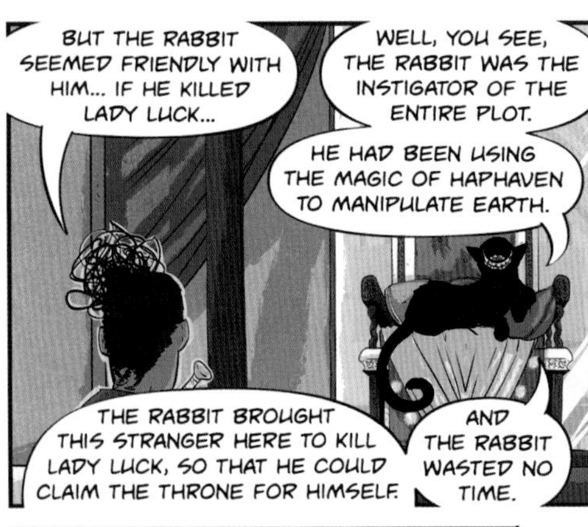
BUT THE RABBIT SEEMED FRIENDLY WITH HIM... IF HE KILLED LADY LUCK...
WELL, YOU SEE, THE RABBIT WAS THE INSTIGATOR OF THE ENTIRE PLOT.
HE HAD BEEN USING THE MAGIC OF HAPHAVEN TO MANIPULATE EARTH.
THE RABBIT BROUGHT THIS STRANGER HERE TO KILL LADY LUCK, SO THAT HE COULD CLAIM THE THRONE FOR HIMSELF.
AND THE RABBIT WASTED NO TIME.

HE TRIED TO STEAL THE CROWN. IT WAS ONLY MY INTERVENTION THAT STOPPED HIM FROM TAKING CONTROL OF HAPHAVEN.

THE JINX GRABBED THE RABBIT AND RAN.
NATURALLY THE KINGDOM WAS ROCKED BY THIS NEWS. I WAS LEFT WITH NO CHOICE BUT TO STEP UP AND ACCEPT THE THRONE MYSELF, SO THAT I COULD SOMEHOW RETURN THE KINGDOM I LOVE TO A SEMBLANCE OF PEACE AND NORMALCY.

AND THAT MEANS THAT PUNISHING THE RABBIT IS MY DUTY.
OUR DUTY, ALEX.

WHEN ZANE MILLS STRUCK LADY LUCK DOWN IN A VIOLENT RAGE, IT CURSED HIS WHOLE BLOODLINE.
YOU HAVE TO BALANCE THE SCALE.
YOU HAVE A DEBT TO PAY.

WHEN A MEMBER OF ZANE'S BLOODLINE SLICES INTO THAT TRAITOR, JUSTICE WILL BE SERVED.
AND THE SEVERE MISFORTUNE THAT PLAGUES YOUR FAMILY WILL BE EASED. YOUR MOTHER WILL BE RESTORED.

OBEY THE SUPERSTITIONS, FOLLOW THEM TO THE LETTER, AND ALL WILL BE RIGHT IN BOTH OF OUR WORLDS.
DO YOU THINK YOU CAN DO THAT?

THE RABBIT'S FATE IS ABOUT JUSTICE, NOT TORTURE. WE GOTTA MAKE SURE YOU CAN DO IT CLEAN.
THAT'S WHY WE'VE SET UP THIS PRACTICE DUMMY.
THE INTERIOR OF WHICH HAS BEEN REINFORCED WITH A MOCK-SKELETON.

A SKELETON?
AYE. THE TRICKY PART OF YOUR TASK IS GOING TO BE GETTING THROUGH THE BONE IN ONE BLOW.
WHAT DO I USE?

WE TOOK THIS FROM THE JINX.

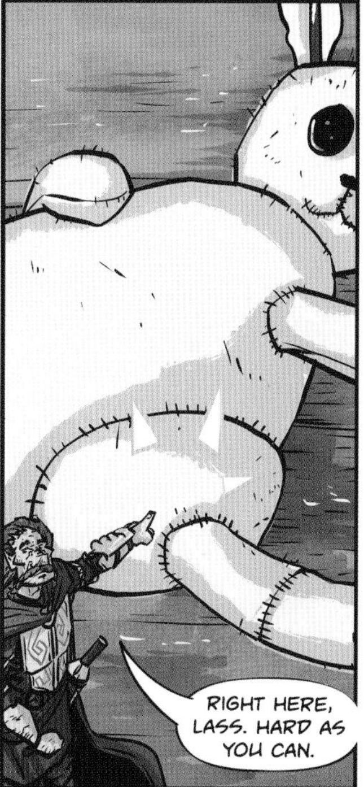
RIGHT HERE, LASS. HARD AS YOU CAN.

THUNK

THAT WON'T DO. THAT'LL JUST HURT HIM.
AND THE BLOOD WILL MAKE IT HARDER TO SEE YOUR TARGET SPOT ON THE NEXT TRY.

AGAIN. HARDER.

HARDER!

THAT'S THE WAY!

I CAN'T DO IT.
IT'S TOO MUCH.
PLEASE, THERE HAS TO BE ANOTHER WAY.

ALEX, I'VE EXPLAINED THIS. THERE IS NO OTHER WAY. BUT I UNDERSTAND. IT'S A HARD THING TO ASK OF ANYONE, LET ALONE A YOUNG WOMAN SUCH AS YOURSELF.
LET ME MAKE ARRANGEMENTS FOR YOU IN THE CASTLE TONIGHT.

AND PERHAPS IN THE MORNING, WITH A FULL BELLY AND A GOOD NIGHT'S REST, YOU'LL SEE THE WAY FORWARD MORE CLEARLY.
THIS WAY, LASS.

DO YOU LIKE THOSE?
TROPHIES.

ZANE'S HORSE?

WELL, WHAT CAN I SAY? HE CROSSED ME.

WHAT'S ON YOUR MIND, ALEX?
MY DAD.
WHEN HE TAUGHT ME ABOUT THE SUPERSTITIONS, HE TAUGHT ME ABOUT STUFF LIKE NUMEROLOGY, AND--
NUMEROLOGY?
OKAY SO, LIKE, WHERE I COME FROM, HANGING A HORSESHOE ABOVE YOUR DOOR IS LUCKY.
PARTIALLY BECAUSE IT HAS SEVEN NAIL HOLES.
WHY SHOULD THAT MATTER?
I DON'T KNOW, IT JUST DID. I THOUGHT.
Wow.
How do they expect me to eat after "target practice?"
WHAT'S THIS?

JUST WATCHING OUT FOR YOU.
I TOLD YOU MY MEN AND I WOULD PROTECT YOU.

YEAH. I FEEL SUPER SAFE RIGHT NOW.

BIT OF ADVICE, ALEX. DON'T THINK ON IT TOO LONG. THINGS'LL GO EASIER FOR US ALL IF YOU DO WHAT NEEDS DOING.

FOR SURE.
"What needs doing."
That's what I'm trying to figure out.

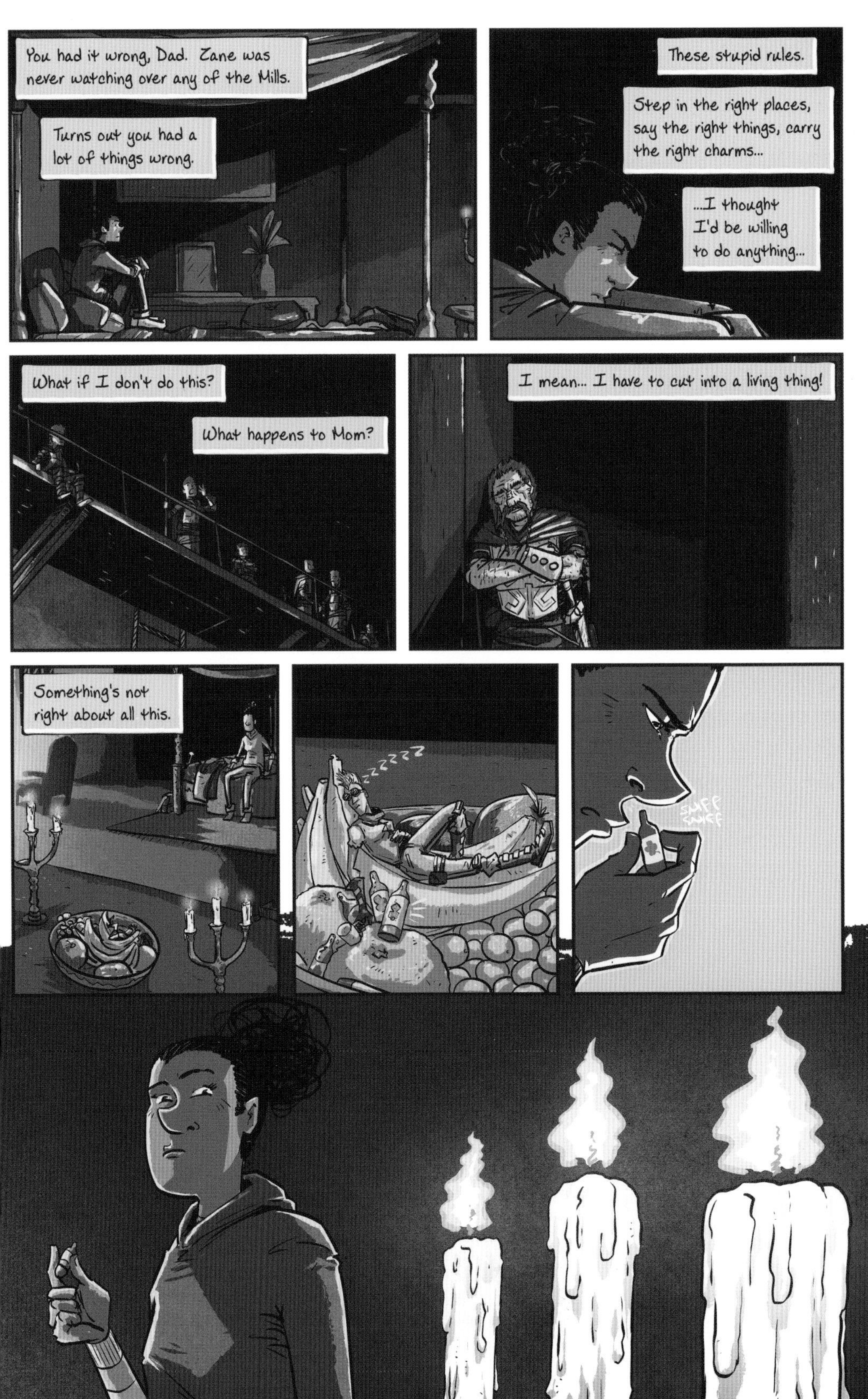
You had it wrong, Dad. Zane was never watching over any of the Mills.
Turns out you had a lot of things wrong.
These stupid rules.
Step in the right places, say the right things, carry the right charms...
...I thought I'd be willing to do anything...
What if I don't do this?
What happens to Mom?
I mean... I have to cut into a living thing!
Something's not right about all this.
ZZZZZZ
SNIFF SNIFF

FIRE!

WHAT IN THE...
SHHH.

THE DUNGEONS, WHERE ARE THEY?
I WANT TO TALK TO ZANE.

THAT WAY.

AHHH!

NO!
PLEASE!
MMMMPH!
MMMMPH!

MY DAD TOLD ME YOU WENT LOOKING FOR LADY LUCK TO FIND OUT WHY THE FISHHOOKS FAILED YOU.
THE CAT TOLD ME YOU WERE LOOKING FOR REVENGE. THAT YOU KILLED HER.
WHAT REALLY HAPPENED?

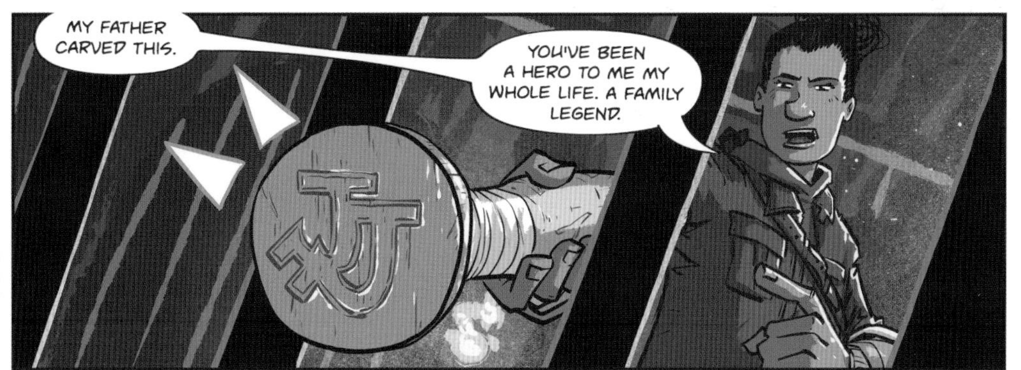
MY FATHER CARVED THIS.
YOU'VE BEEN A HERO TO ME MY WHOLE LIFE. A FAMILY LEGEND.

MY NAME IS ALEXANDRIA ZANE MILLS.
I'M YOUR GREAT-GREAT GRANDDAUGHTER.

WASN'T ME THAT STABBED LADY LUCK.

IT WOULD MAKE SENSE. YOU'D LOST EVERYTHING. YOU'D UNDERSTANDABLY BE UPSET. MAYBE UNBALANCED.
GIRL, DON'T YOU ACCUSE ME AGAIN!

ZANE'S TELLING THE TRUTH. I WAS THERE.
I HEARD YOU WERE PART OF IT.
WELL IT WOULDN'T BE A VERY GOOD LIE IF I WASN'T ACCOUNTED FOR, WOULD IT?

S'LIKE YOUR FATHER SAID. I WAS DOWN AND OUT. I FELT CURSED.
AND IT DROVE ME TO SEEK OUT LADY LUCK.
I SPENT YEARS LOOKING FOR HER. TALKED WITH MYSTICS. SMOKED WITH SHAMANS. TOOK A VOYAGE 'CROSS THE SEA. CHASED EVERY CLUE I COULD. EVERY GHOST STORY. EVERY TALL TALE. BUT FINALLY I FOUND IT...

...THE END OF THE RAINBOW.

AND THEY WELCOMED ME.

I HADN'T BEEN IN THE THRONE ROOM BUT MAYBE TWO MINUTES WHEN SUDDENLY, WITH NO WARNING AT ALL, THE CAT LEAPT UP AND DROVE A BLADE INTO LADY LUCK'S CHEST.
HE MOVED FAST. DIDN'T HESITATE.

THEN HE TURNED ON THE RABBIT. AGAIN, NO HESITATION.
THIS WAS SOMETHING HE'D BEEN PLANNING.
BUT SOMETHING WAS WRONG.

THE CAT COULDN'T KILL ME. NOT AS IN, "HE COULDN'T BRING HIMSELF TO DO IT."
HE WAS ACTUALLY, PHYSICALLY UNABLE TO PERFORM THE TASK.
THE CAT AND I, WE'RE TWO SIDES OF THE SAME COIN. FORTUNE AND MISFORTUNE. WE CAN'T HARM EACH OTHER. WE DIDN'T KNOW IT THEN, BECAUSE WE'D NEVER TRIED...

...I MEAN, WHY WOULD WE, RIGHT? THAT WOULD BE **INSANE**.
OH YEAH, TURNS OUT ONE OF US IS.
MURDEROUSLY INSANE.

SO THERE'S ME, FUMBLIN' AND SLACK-JAWED, WATCHIN' THIS TALKING CAT RAIN DOWN CHAOS ON HIS FRIENDS. THOUGHT I'D LOST MY MIND.

ONCE I FINALLY SHOOK MYSELF OUT OF MY STUPOR, I TRIED TO HELP.

DID THE ONLY THING I COULD THINK OF.
AND THE CAT RETALIATED.

JINX.
BLAM

I WAS PANICKED, FRIGHTENED. I GRABBED OL' LONG EARS AND TOOK TO RUNNIN'.
EVERYONE IN THE CITY SAW A GIANT MONSTER DRAGGING ME OUT OF THE CASTLE AND OFF INTO THE WOODS, LEAVING A MURDERED LADY LUCK BEHIND. NO ONE KNEW WHAT HAD REALLY HAPPENED.

WE'VE SPENT THE LAST CENTURY IN SLUGWOOD, FENDING OFF THE CAT'S FORCES AND JUST TRYING TO STAY ALIVE.
WHY NOT TRY AND CLEAR YOUR NAMES? OR FIGHT BACK?

LOOK AT ME. LOOK AT WHAT HAPPENS YOU CROSS THE CAT.
AIN'T NO FIGHT WE CAN WIN.
ONLY OPTION I HAD WAS TO TRY AND KEEP THE RABBIT SAFE SO THAT I DIDN'T HAVE TO WATCH ANOTHER LIFE END BECAUSE OF ME.

"ANOTHER LIFE END..." OH BOY..
ZANE, YOU MELODRAMATIC LUG... YOU'RE INNOCENT, REMEMBER?
NAH, I AIN'T INNOCENT. I DIDN'T STAB LADY LUCK, BUT IT IS MY FAULT SHE'S DEAD.

MY LAST GAME... I KNEW THE BANDIT THAT BEAT ME. KNEW HIS TELLS. I COULD SEE HE WAS HOLDIN' A KILLER HAND. BUT I COULDN'T ADMIT TO MYSELF THAT THE FISHHOOKS MIGHT FAIL ME, SO I WENT ALL IN.
IF I'D HAVE FOLDED LIKE I SHOULDA... I WOULDN'T BE HERE.
AND IF I HADN'T COME HERE, LADY LUCK'D STILL BE--

DEAD, ZANE. SHE'D STILL BE DEAD.
THE CAT WOULD HAVE FOUND ANOTHER OPPORTUNITY.
YOU DIDN'T HAVE ANY CONTROL OVER IT.
IT WASN'T YOUR FAULT.

BUT IF I DON'T HAVE A BLOOD DEBT TO PAY... WHAT ABOUT MY MOM AND YOUR FOOT?
WHAT EXACTLY IS IT THAT AILS YOUR MOMMA?
I STEPPED ON A CRACK.

AND?

"STEP ON A CRACK, BREAK YOUR MOTHER'S BACK."
NEVER HEARD OF THAT.
WHAT? BUT...

ALL THE OTHER SUPERSTITIONS COME FROM HAPHAVEN.
KNOCKING ON WOOD, PICKING UP PENNIES, HANGING UP HORSESHOES.
IT'S ALL BEHAVIOR IN THIS WORLD. SO WHAT BREAKS BACKS IN HAPHAVEN?
NOTHING SPECIFIC. BACKS ARE BREAKABLE. OF COURSE. BUT THERE'S NO REGULAR BEHAVIOR OR CUSTOM... NOT LIKE THE OTHER THINGS YOU MENTION...

WAIT, ACTUALLY THAT'S NOT ENTIRELY TRUE...
...THERE'S LAW.

LAW?
OBVIOUSLY, EARTH AND HAPHAVEN SHARE A BOND. OUR BEHAVIORS CREATE AN IMPACT ON THE PEOPLE OF EARTH WHO MIRROR THEM.
FOR DECADES WE HAD A TEAM OF TOP LEPRECHAUN MINDS STUDYING THE LINK. AND THE CAT WAS FASCINATED BY THEIR RESEARCH.

TURNS OUT, HE WAS EVEN GOING IN FOR PRIVATE LECTURES EVERY NOW AND AGAIN. THE SCIENTISTS DIDN'T SUSPECT ANYTHING. THEY THOUGHT IT WAS JUST GENUINE SCIENTIFIC CURIOSITY. THE CAT WAS ALREADY AN ARCHEOLOGY BUFF, SO IT DIDN'T SEEM STRANGE THAT HE'D PURSUE THIS, TOO.

AND THEN ONE DAY THE CAT PITCHES THIS IDEA THAT EARTH COULD BE ***CONTROLLED*** BY HAPHAVEN LAWS.

HE WANTED TO ***WEAPONIZE*** SUPERSTITION.

LADY LUCK REFUSED.

BUT THE CAT'S ON THE THRONE NOW. AND HIS DECREES ARE LAW. HE WANTS ME HURT, AND HE CAN'T DO IT HIMSELF. SO HE'S LOOKING TO CONTROL SOMEONE.

YOU THINK THE CAT WROTE A LAW ABOUT MY MOM, JUST SO THAT I'D HURT YOU?

WELL, AS YOU CAN IMAGINE, I HAVEN'T EXACTLY BEEN ABLE TO GO OVER THE BOOKS IN THE LAST HUNDRED YEARS, BUT... YEAH, IT WOULD BE POSSIBLE. AND JUST LIKE HIM TO DO IT.

THIS IS SO TERRIBLY DISAPPOINTING.

WHEN HUBBUB TOLD ME YOU'D RUN DOWN HERE, ALEX, I ALLOWED MYSELF THE BRIEFEST MOMENT OF HAPPINESS. I HOPED YOU'D COME TO YOUR SENSES AND WERE ABOUT TO PERFORM A BIT OF LEPORINE PODIATRY.

"LEPORINE PODIATRY." THIS GUY.

A HUNDRED YEARS LATER AND YOU'RE NOT ANY DIFFERENT. SO INSECURE IN YOUR OWN SKIN YOU HAVE TO CUT EVERYONE DOWN, EVEN IF IT'S JUST FOR THEIR--
ME CUT EVERYONE DOWN? YOU DERANGED HAIRBALL, YOU'RE *LITERALLY* TRYING TO--

ENOUGH!

DID YOU DO WHAT THE RABBIT SAYS?
DID YOU EXPLOIT THE BOND WITH EARTH TO FORCE ME INTO THIS?

YES.
I DID.
I HAD TO.
THAT'S THE THING ABOUT BEING KING--I HAVE TO UPHOLD LAW AND ORDER. AND IF THE RABBIT GOES UNPUNISHED, THERE IS NO ORDER.

AND THE RABBIT'S RIGHT... I CAN'T HARM HIM MYSELF.
THAT IS THE ONE PIECE OF MAGIC IN HAPHAVEN MORE POWERFUL THAN THE KING. I CAN'T EVEN ORDER A LEPRECHAUN TO DO IT.
SO, YES, I DID NEED TO... MOTIVATE YOU.

MOTIVATE ME?!
BY ATTACKING MY MOM?

JUST CUT THE RABBIT, ALEX.
I HAVE WORKED SO HARD TO GET US TO THIS POINT, YOU REALLY HAVE NO IDEA.

THE PAIR OF JACKS THAT FAILED ZANE... THAT WAS YOU, TOO, WASN'T IT? YOU USED HAPHAVEN TO GIVE HIM A LIFETIME OF FORTUNE, AND THEN RIPPED IT OUT FROM UNDER HIM. TO DRAW HIM HERE. SO YOU'D HAVE SOMEONE TO FRAME.
A STRANGER, WHO NO ONE IN HAPHAVEN COULD VOUCH FOR.
BUT WHEN YOU FOUND OUT YOU COULDN'T HURT THE RABBIT, YOU HAD TO BAIT SOMEONE ELSE. SO...

OH GOD...
MY DAD... DID YOU...

YOUR POOR FATHER. I HEARD ABOUT HIM.
AN ODDLY UNSEASONABLE RAINY NIGHT, A MALFUNCTIONING ALARM, AND A FELLED POWER LINE.

OF ALL THE ROTTEN LUCK.

FIX MY MOM RIGHT NOW, OR SO HELP ME--
YOU AND ZANE CERTAINLY ARE RELATED, AREN'T YOU? NEITHER ONE OF YOU KNOWS HOW TO PLAY THE CARDS YOU'RE HOLDING.
DO NOT CROSS ME, ALEX.

FIX HER!

JINX.

I'M SORRY, ALEX, BUT YOU FORCED MY HAND, YOU REALLY DID.
I THOUGHT YOU'D SEE REASON, BUT IT'S CLEAR I HAVE TO RAISE THE STAKES. "GO ALL IN," TO BORROW A PHRASE.
SO LET'S MAKE A FORMAL AMENDMENT TO THE LAW ABOUT YOUR MOTHER...

...YOU NOW HAVE UNTIL SUNRISE TO GIVE ME THE RABBIT'S FOOT OR YOUR MOTHER'S CONDITION WILL BECOME TERMINAL.
YOU'RE FIGHTING FOR HER LIFE NOW, ALEX. DO TRY AND MANAGE TO SAVE AT LEAST ONE PARENT.

SEAL THE MAIN DOOR AND THEN OPEN THEIR CELLS.
LET THEM MINGLE.

I EXPECT ALEX WILL DO EXACTLY AS SHE'S TOLD NOW.

CLANG
OH, DEAR. ALEX...

A HISTORY OF HAPHAVEN

by Smidgen Stonewick – Keeper of History, First Order

Entry 418 – "The Jinx"

Zane transformed into the Jinx as punishment for slaying Lady Luck. But no Haphaven monarch in modern history had ever been so brutally attacked and, we lack precedent for the instigation of such a curse. But there is evidence that Zane is not the first Jinx to walk upon Haphaven soil.

During the Golden Age of Haphaven, archeologists studied ruins in the center of Slugwood Forest dating back to before the arrival of Leprechauns in Haphaven. There they found records of an old and ancient race which once did battle with monsters believed to be Jinxes. These artifacts were collected by the Black Cat during his time as an advisor, to be safely preserved within the castle vaults. And while that exhausts the limits of what we know of Jinx history, a careful and long-distance observation of Zane Mills has allowed for some modern examination of the Jinx, who now makes his home amongst those same ruins.

The torrential downpour is the most often noted aspect. A singular storm cloud locked over the Jinx's head leads to a sad, soggy existence tinged with musty, moldy odors. And occasional bolts of lightning surge painfully through the Jinx's body.

The Jinx is also burdened with itchy, wart-covered skin. Eyes extra sensitive to light. Ravenous hunger. Uncontrollable rage. And, worst of all, a loss of control over his fate--his tools no longer work properly, his efforts are rife with spontaneous error.

Could anything in either realm truly be as heinous as that?

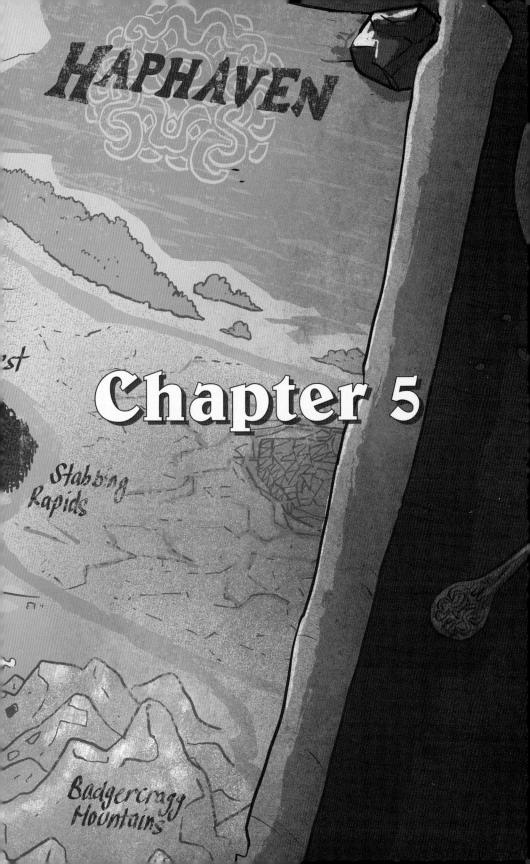

Chapter 5

God.
What've I done?
DOES IT HURT? ARE YOU OKAY?
ALEX?

My only choice... I have to follow the superstition...

ALEX...

Do it! Don't be a coward... It's your only choice...

...PLEASE...

Mom.

...DO IT...

WHAT?

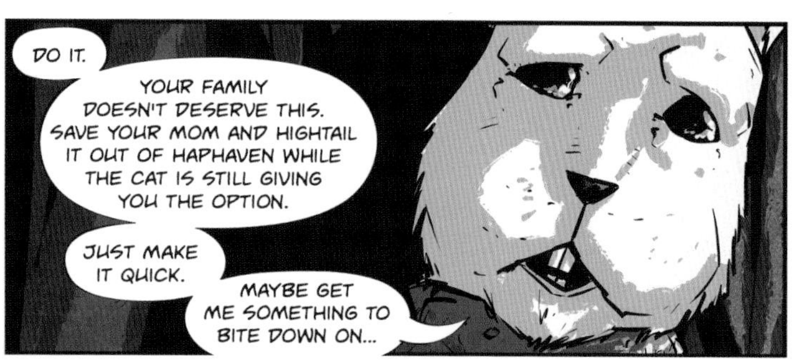
DO IT.
YOUR FAMILY DOESN'T DESERVE THIS. SAVE YOUR MOM AND HIGHTAIL IT OUT OF HAPHAVEN WHILE THE CAT IS STILL GIVING YOU THE OPTION.
JUST MAKE IT QUICK.
MAYBE GET ME SOMETHING TO BITE DOWN ON...

Do it!
What is wrong with me?
Follow the superstition!
Okay... just like "target practice..."
DO IT... FOR YOUR MOM...

YOUR MOMMA! OF COURSE! I PLUM NEAR FORGOT...
ALEX, NO! HOLD ON, GIRL! WAIT JUST A SEC... I GOT...

ALEX!
LOOK.

WHAT?

WE TOOK IT FROM YOU EARLIER, BUT... LOOK, LOOK, IT'S FOR YOU.

I DON'T UNDERSTAND...

IT'S FROM YOUR MOMMA. IT'S A NOTE. FOR YOU.

SORRY ABOUT OPENIN' IT.
HAD TO MAKE SURE IT WAS, UH... YOU KNOW, NOT FROM THE KING OR ANYTHING.
THERE WAS A BLACK CAT ON THE ENVELOPE... WE SUSPECTED...
...
SORRY.

Dear Alex,

I know you've said you don't want to make a fuss this year. But you and I both know I won't let it go. So we're probably going to have another fight about it.

And if I remember being a moody thirteen-year-old correctly, I'd be willing to bet that there's a better than average chance that you won't be speaking to me on the morning of your actual birthday.

So I'm writing this now and slipping the card into your jacket before all that goes down.

Hopefully you find it at school and it embarrasses you in front of that Matt guy you have a crush on. Serves you right.

Let me say now that this argument I'm predicting--it isn't entirely your fault. You're not the only one still working through the loss of your father.

I'm supposed to be strong for you. I'm not supposed to admit things like this. But on the inside, I feel just as lost as you do.

There's a story I've never told you about your father.

I've tried a couple of times, but I can't bring myself to for fear of breaking down and blubbering and ruining the illusion that I'm your super strong pillar.

Your dad was superstitious from the day I met him.
It was Christmas time, and I was trapped in this mall. Late for work and on my last nerve.
I saw a shortcut.
I went for it.
And out of nowhere pops this guy with some corny line about the danger of walking under ladders.
At least, I thought it was just a corny line. But as we talked I realized he was serious. Like, completely serious. He was convinced he'd just saved my life or something.
I missed work that day. Had a coffee date instead. It was worth it.

A couple of years later, when we found out you were on the way, your father began work on the nursery.
He hung horseshoes over the door. He painted a mural of rainbows and four-leaf clovers on the wall.
Our doctor only just managed to talk him out of spraying the room down with clover essence or something equally bizarre. I can't remember now.
But he took it all as seriously as he took that ladder. He wasn't just decorating a room for you. He was building a fortress of good fortune to protect his child.
But when he held you for the first time in his arms, everything changed.
We brought you home and he took it all down.
Horseshoes--gone.
Mural--painted over.
Sure, he never gave up his superstitions entirely. But it was all trivial. Pregame rituals for softball and a rabbit's foot on his key chain.
None of it was good enough to protect you.
From the moment he first stared into your eyes, he knew he couldn't hand over the responsibility for your safety to four-leaf clovers or Zane or anything else. He had to take control of it.
You meant that much to him.

And you mean that much to me. And I want you to mean that much to yourself.
Zane Mills had lucky cards. But I think Alex Mills is smart enough and talented enough to win with whatever cards come her way.
Happy birthday, Alex.
SLUGGER
Love always, Mom
I'VE BEEN HANDLING THIS ALL WRONG.

THE WHOLE REASON I'M EVEN HERE IS BECAUSE I'M TRYING TO SAVE SOMEONE WHO DOESN'T ABIDE BY ANY OF THIS.
I'M TRYING TO SAVE SOMEONE WHO, IF THE SITUATION WAS REVERSED, WOULD BURN THIS CASTLE TO THE GROUND.
BUT, ALEX, YOU'VE ALREADY LOST... AIN'T NOTHING YOU CAN DO NOW.

WHY NOT?
IF YOU CROSS THE CAT--
I ALREADY HAVE, ZANE.

BUT THINK ABOUT IT. IT'S ONLY BAD LUCK TO CROSS THE BLACK CAT, BECAUSE EVERYONE WHO HAS CROSSED HIM HAS LOST. IF YOU CROSS HIM AND WIN...
FORTUNE CHANGES.
WE'RE IN FREAKING SUPERSTITION TOWN. THIS IS WHERE THE RULES ARE MADE. IF WE TAKE CONTROL OF OUR SITUATION, THEN WE CAN WRITE NEW RULES.
WE CAN LITERALLY MAKE OUR OWN LUCK.

Mom wouldn't let this Jinx thing stop her.
Let's try this her way.
EVERYONE, AWAY FROM THE DOOR.

ALEX?

I DON'T GET IT. WHAT'S SHE DOING?

ZANE, CAN YOU DO THAT? WHY HAVEN'T YOU EVER DONE THAT?
THE HISTORY KEEPERS WILL WRITE ABOUT THIS...
LET'S GO GET MY GUNS.

WE HAVE UNTIL SUNRISE TO GET THAT CROWN OFF THE CAT AND APPOINT THE RABBIT AS RULER OF HAPHAVEN.
WE DO THAT AND YOU'LL CURE MY MOM. RIGHT?
INDUBITABLY.

AND, HEY, LISTEN... SORRY ABOUT THE...
DON'T MENTION IT.

LET'S SKIN US A CAT.

GET HIS HIGHNESS TO SAFETY!

GET THE KING INTO THE THRONE ROOM! GO!

GRAB

EASY NOW, PENNY.
I THINK YOU AND I SHOULD HAVE A TALK.
I SUSPECT I'M IN OVER MY HEAD.
I WANT TO KNOW EVERY WORD THAT WAS SPOKEN IN THAT DUNGEON BEFORE WE ARRIVED.

STAND BACK! I'LL TRY TO LIGHTNING THROUGH THE DOOR AGAIN.
HOLD UP, I GOT THIS... I THINK. JUST GIMME A SEC...

WHAT'S GOING ON?! WHERE IS HUBBUB?
DON'T WORRY, YOUR HIGHNESS. THEY'LL NEVER BREACH THIS--

TOLD YOU.

NICE WORK, FISHHOOKS.
SHOW SOME RESPECT, GIRL.
THAT AIN'T NO WAY TO REFER TO YOUR GRANDPAPPY.
Grandpappy.
CAT'LL BE CORNERED IN THE THRONE ROOM. WE GOT HIM.
GO TEAM MILLS!

TICKTOCK, ALEX.

WHAT THE--

GET BACK HERE!
CRACK!

STAND BACK, 'LEX.
I THOUGHT THERE'D BE A TUNNEL OR...
COME ON, WE'LL FIND ANOTHER WAY.

I BELIEVE WE'VE REACHED AN UNDERSTANDING.

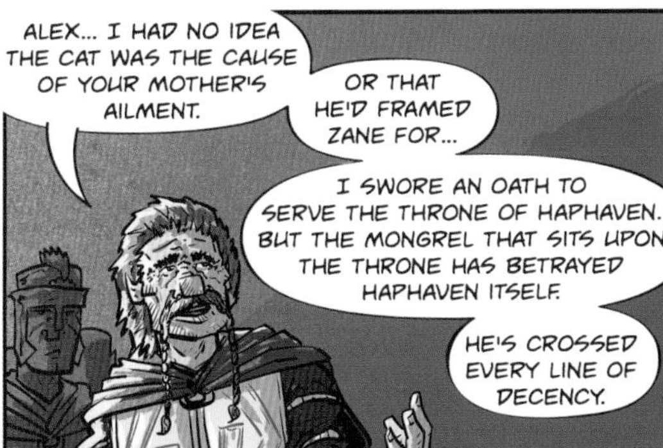
ALEX... I HAD NO IDEA THE CAT WAS THE CAUSE OF YOUR MOTHER'S AILMENT.
OR THAT HE'D FRAMED ZANE FOR...
I SWORE AN OATH TO SERVE THE THRONE OF HAPHAVEN. BUT THE MONGREL THAT SITS UPON THE THRONE HAS BETRAYED HAPHAVEN ITSELF.
HE'S CROSSED EVERY LINE OF DECENCY.

THANK YOU, HUBBUB.
HELP US OUT. THE CAT SLIPPED AWAY.
THROUGH A MIRROR. DOES THAT MAKE SENSE?

ENCHANTED MIRROR. IMMEDIATE TELEPORTATION FOR EMERGENCY ESCAPES.
THE CAT INSTALLED IT AFTER HE TOOK CONTROL. PUT A PENALTY OF SEVEN YEARS IN THE DUNGEON FOR ANYONE WHO DARED TAMPER WITH IT.
HE CAN PUT IT ON OUR TAB.

WHERE'S IT LEAD--

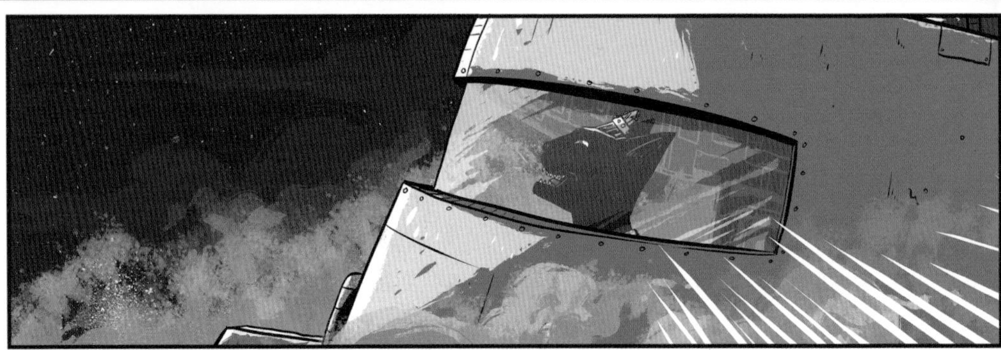

WE HAVE TO FOLLOW HIM!
THAT'S THE *LEVIATHAN*. KING'S PERSONAL AIRSHIP. FASTEST IN THE FLEET. WE CAN PREP A CRAFT TO FOLLOW HIM, BUT IT'LL BE A FUTILE EFFORT.

GRAB

BLAM
BLAM
BLAM

YOU AIN'T GONNA BRING THE SHIP DOWN THAT WAY.
BLAM
BLAM
BLAM

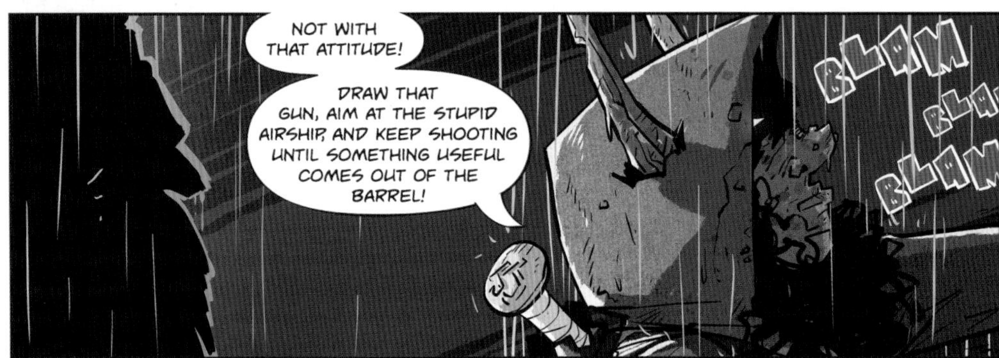
NOT WITH THAT ATTITUDE!
DRAW THAT GUN, AIM AT THE STUPID AIRSHIP, AND KEEP SHOOTING UNTIL SOMETHING USEFUL COMES OUT OF THE BARREL!
BLAM
BLAM

THAT'S NOT WHAT I MEAN, 'LEX. YOU GOTTA DO LIKE YOU DID BACK IN THE DUNGEON.

CONCENTRATE. TAKE CONTROL.

CLICK

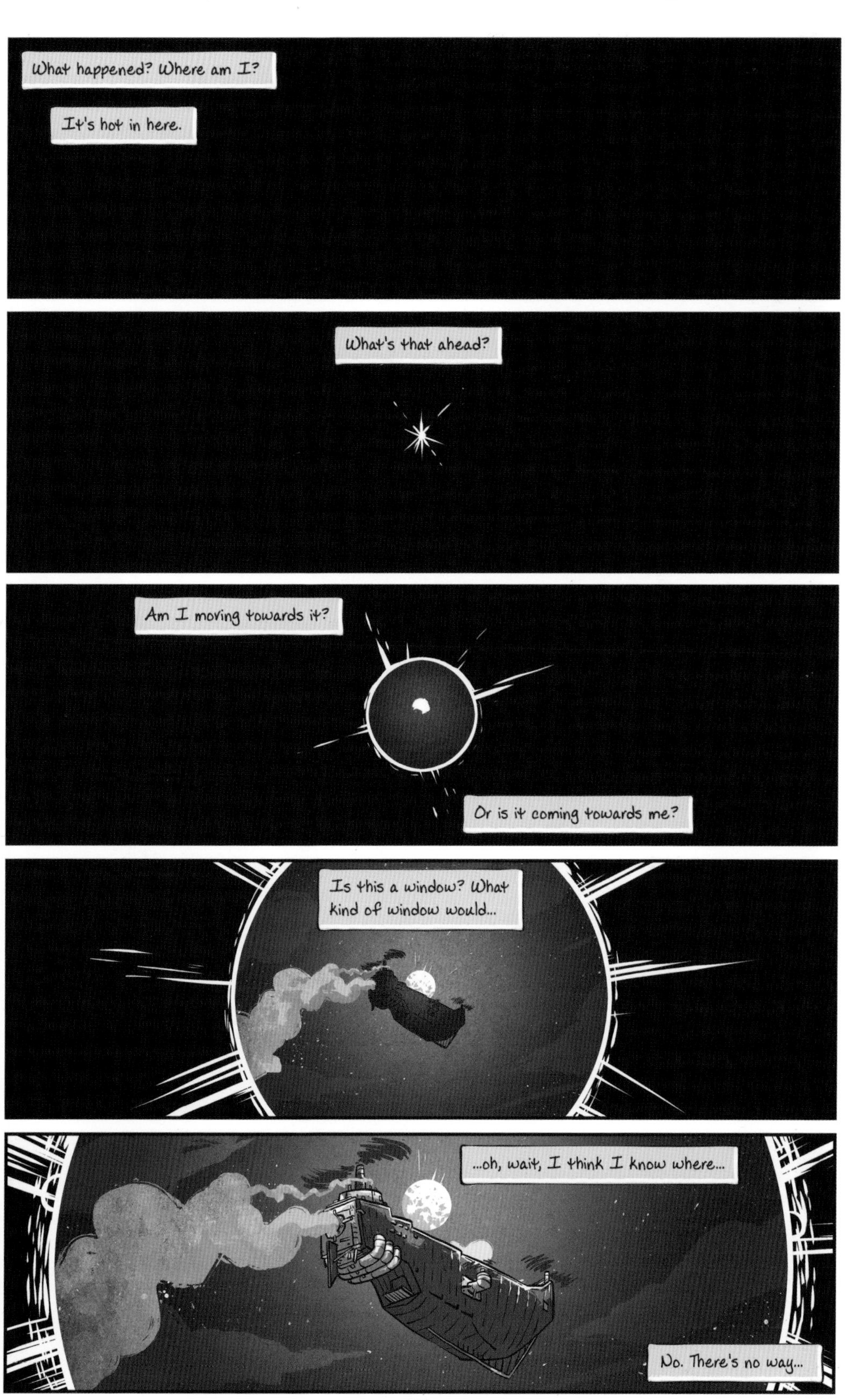
What happened? Where am I?
It's hot in here.
What's that ahead?
Am I moving towards it?
Or is it coming towards me?
Is this a window? What kind of window would...
...oh, wait, I think I know where...
No. There's no way...

...NO FLIPPIN' WAY!

THUNK

That was awe--

Whoa!

If I can just get to the top...
...I think I can balance it back out.

YOU AND YOU.
WITH ME.

HOLD UP NOW, WHERE YOU OFF TO?
AIRSHIP. I WANT TO FOLLOW THEM.
YOU SAID THERE AIN'T NO WAY YOU CAN CATCH UP.

IT'S A GOOD STRATEGY. WE DON'T NEED TO CATCH UP COMPLETELY. BUT ALEX NEEDS TO GET THE CROWN ON THE RABBIT'S HEAD BY SUNRISE...
...SO WE NEED TO KEEP THE RABBIT AS CLOSE TO THE CROWN AS POSSIBLE. SHORTEN ALEX'S RETURN TRIP, IF WE CAN.

SORRY 'BOUT THIS NOW, BUT THE RABBIT'S UNDER MY PROTECTION AND--

ZANE. YOU'VE KEPT ME SAFE FOR A CENTURY. YOU'VE DONE YOUR PART.

I'VE PUT THIS OFF FOR TOO LONG. I GOTTA JOB TO DO, WHETHER I WANT IT OR NOT.

WHAT WILL IT TAKE, ALEX?

IF THE THREAT OF YOUR MOTHER'S LIFE WON'T MOTIVATE YOU, HOW ABOUT THE WORLD?
DO YOU REALIZE THE POWER I HAVE? I CAN DECREE THAT THE NEXT TIME A BABY SNEEZES, EARTH'S COLLECTIVE NUCLEAR ARSENAL WILL LAUNCH.

YOU COULD. BUT YOU WON'T.
PUSH ME AND FIND OUT.

DESTROY EARTH AND THERE'LL BE NO ONE LEFT WHO COULD HURT THE RABBIT FOR YOU.
YOU ONLY WANT TO HURT HIM BECAUSE YOU CAN'T.
YOU DON'T WANT ANYTHING AS MUCH AS YOU WANT CONTROL. AND EVERY DAY THAT THE RABBIT GOES UNHARMED IS A DAY YOU HAVE TO DEAL WITH THERE BEING ***SOMETHING*** THAT YOU CAN'T CONTROL.

...
IF IT'S A FIGHT YOU WANT, ALEX, IT'S A FIGHT I'LL GIVE YOU.

DOESN'T HAVE TO BE A FIGHT. THERE IS AN EASY WAY. HAND OVER THE CROWN.
YOU KNOW I WON'T.
SO GO AHEAD, BLAST ME WITH A WATER BALLOON OR A BIRTHDAY CANDLE OR WHATEVER NONSENSICAL TCHOTCHKE THAT GUN IS GOING TO FIRE NEXT.

BLAM

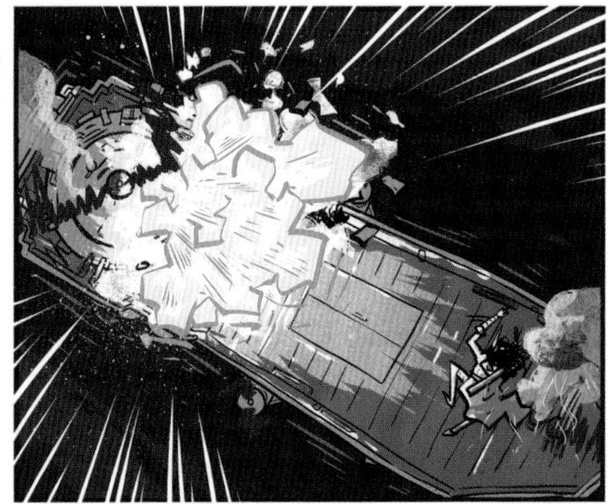

I must've hit part of the engine...

Was that good luck or bad luck?
Like it matters anymore.

There are definitely benefits to being a monster.

YOU STUPID...

...LITTLE...
...TWIT.

DO YOU HAVE ANY IDEA HOW MUCH TIME AND EFFORT AND PLANNING I PUT INTO YOU?!
THE FATE OF GENERATIONS OF THE MILLS FAMILY, CAREFULLY ORCHESTRATED TO MOLD THE PERFECT, SUPERSTITIOUS, RABBIT-SLAUGHTERING WARRIOR INTO EXISTENCE!
SO WHY DO YOU REFUSE TO COOPERATE?!

JUST DO WHAT I TELL YOU TO DO!

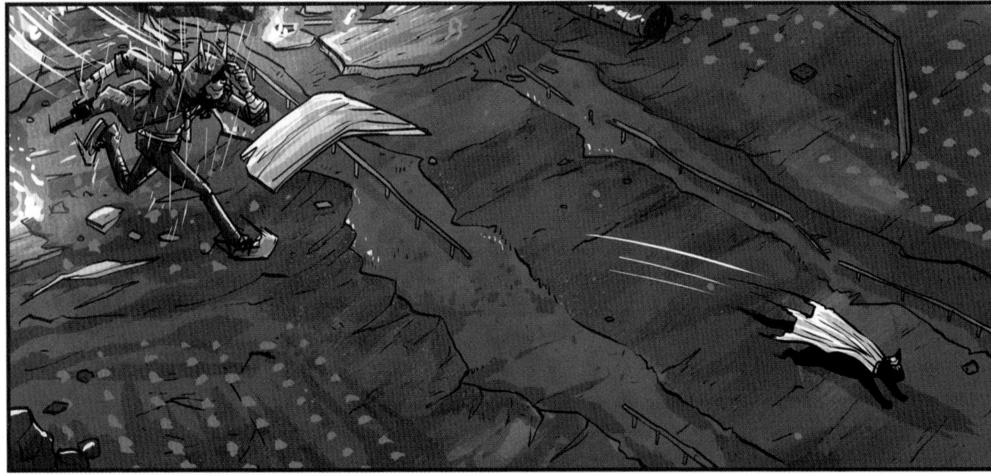

Why does that hurt worse than an airship crash?
I'll never catch the Cat if I have to hit every tree... sun'll be up any minute...

Come on, Alex. Take control.

LISTEN! ATTENTION, ALL OF YOU.

I'M BEING PURSUED BY A JINX! I NEED YOUR HELP!

THERE IT IS! ATTACK IT!
I ORDER YOU TO PROTECT ME!
DEFEND THE CROWN.

EVERYONE STAY BACK. YOU WANT TO PROTECT THE CROWN?
WAIT UNTIL AFTER I'VE PRIED IT OFF OF HIS HEAD.

FINE. I'LL KILL IT MYSELF.
AND THEN I'LL JUST MOLD ANOTHER HUMAN TO COME AND DO MY BIDDING.

YOU HAVEN'T SAVED ANYONE, ALEX!

AHUH-- AHUH--

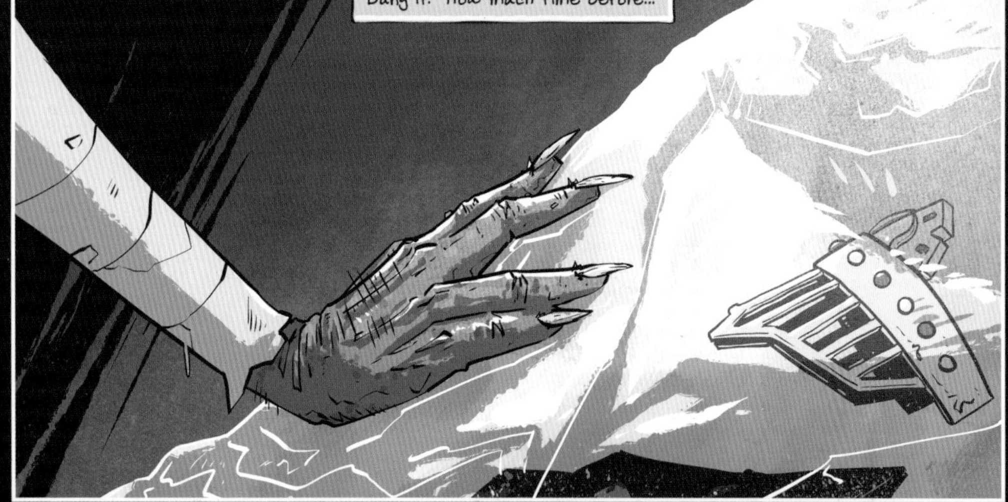
Dang it. How much time before...

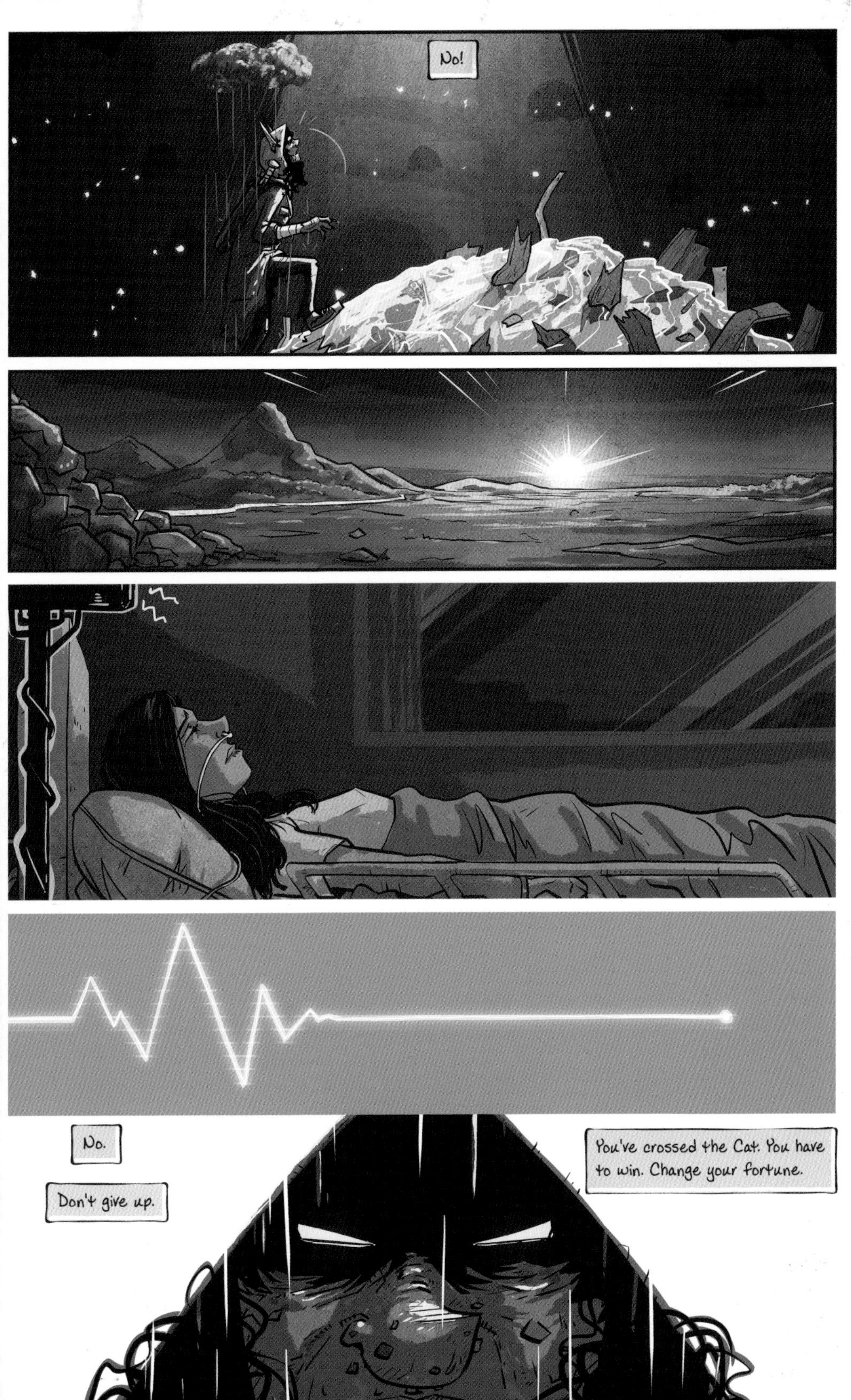
No!
No.
Don't give up.
You've crossed the Cat. You have to win. Change your fortune.

Supposed to get this crown to the Rabbit.

But there's no time.
CRACK

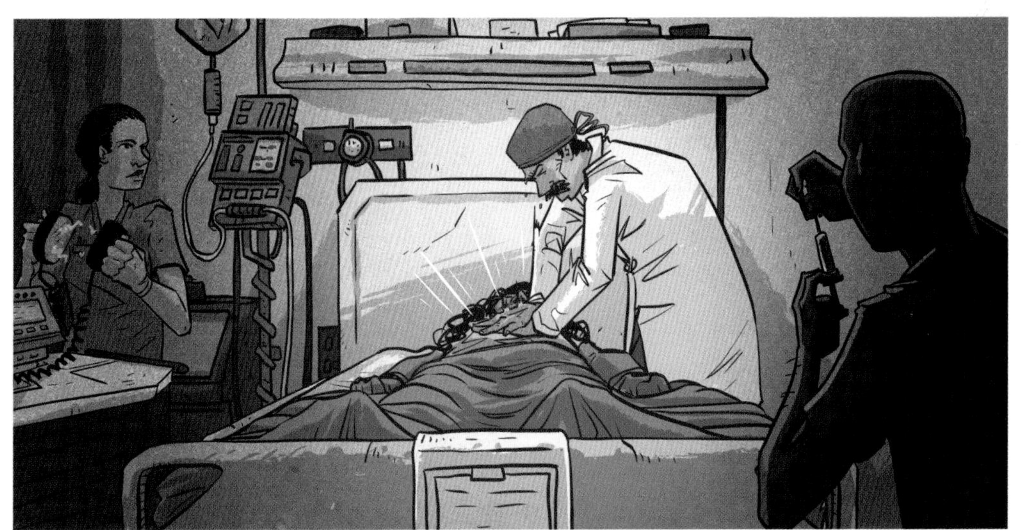

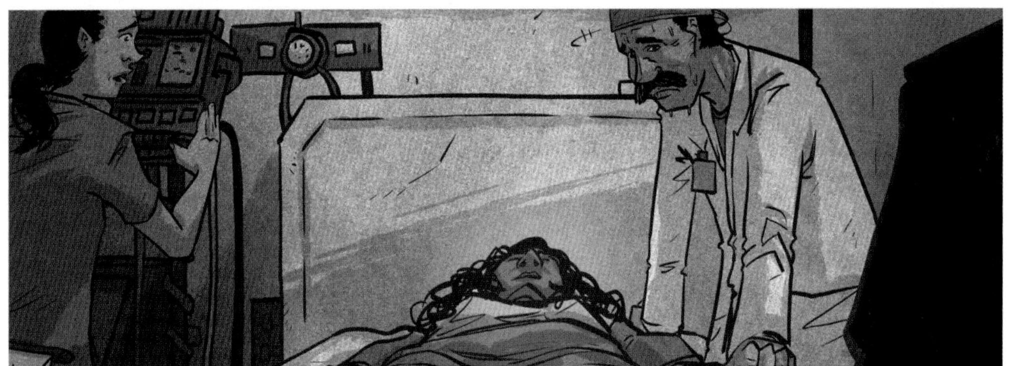
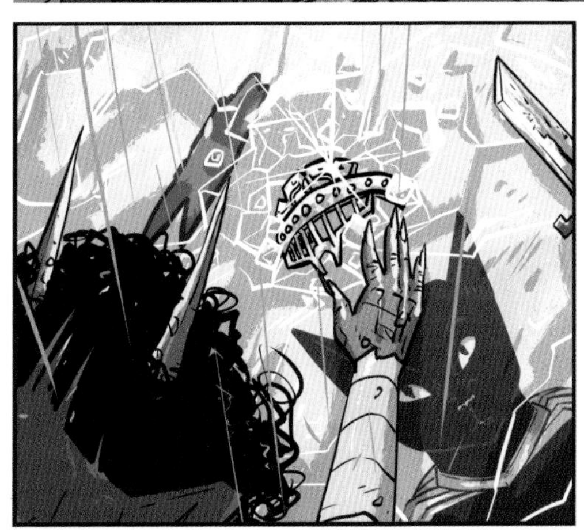

I AM THE RULER OF HAPHAVEN.
AND I DECREE...

AHUH!

WHUP
WHUP

ALEX! OH, DEAR, ARE WE IN TIME?
WHUP

I THINK SO. YEAH.
BUT, UH... SORRY ABOUT YOUR MINE.
AGAIN.
IT'S A LITTLE WORSE THIS TIME...

YOUR HIGHNESS.
YUP. THAT'S ME, I GUESS. UNLESS YOU WANT TO KEEP--
NO.
I JUST WANT TO GO HOME.

THEY'RE GONNA THROW ONE OF THOSE PARTIES, AREN'T THEY?
I HATE THAT STUFF.

AS MY FIRST DECREE...
...OH-BOY...
...I PUT AN END TO THE JINX CURSE.

WHOA!
THAT IS *WEIRD.*

OH, THAT FEELS SO GOOD. YOU HAVE NO IDEA.
I HAD THE CROWN, I DON'T KNOW WHY I DIDN'T--

ZANE, YOU'RE--

AND THAT KIND OF THINKING IS WHY I WANT YOU TO BE ONE OF MY ROYAL ADVISORS.

REALLY? TAKE YOUR OLD PLACE?

WHAT? NO.

THE CAT'S.

GEEZ, MAN, YOU'RE A JINX.

SO WHO'S GONNA TAKE YOUR OLD SPOT?
NO IDEA.
THERE USED TO BE THIS GUY FROM RAVENGLEN, BUT IT'S BEEN A HUNDRED YEARS. I FORGET HIS NAME...

HEY!

SHOULD BE HER.
WHEN YOU'RE IN OVER YOUR HEAD, GET HER ON YOUR SIDE. SHE'LL TURN YOUR FORTUNE AROUND.

BESIDES I KINDA REALLY RUINED THINGS FOR HER AT HER LAST JOB... AGAIN...

DO I LOOK LIKE I'M IN OVER MY HEAD?
I DO, DON'T I?
THEY CAN SENSE IT.
SOMEBODY GET HER SOMETHING TO STAND ON...

LADIES AND GENTLEMEN, I PRESENT TO YOU...

...THE NEW RULER OF HAPHAVEN AND HIS ROYAL ADVISORS!
THIS IS GONNA TAKE SOME GETTING USED TO.
ALRIGHT, MY NEXT DECREE COMES AT THE REQUEST OF A PRETTY LITTLE LADY ALL THE WAY IN FROM OVER THE RAINBOW.
AND SO I DECREE THAT THE CONNECTION BETWEEN HAPHAVEN AND EARTH SHALL BE SEVER--
LET ME STOP YOU RIGHT THERE, YOUR HIGHNESS.
BEFORE YOU DO THAT, WE SHOULD GET ALEX BACK HOME.
RIGHT.
THAT IS AN EXCELLENT IDEA.
SOMEONE MARK HIM DOWN FOR A RAISE.
THIS WAY, LASS.
COME TO THINK OF IT... HOW DO WE CATCH THE RAINBOW FROM THIS END?

IS THAT...?
YUP.
FIRE IT UP, LADS!

JUST STEP ON THROUGH, LASS.
DON'T FIDGET DURING THE RIDE AND YOU'LL TOUCH DOWN GENTLE AS A LEAF AT THE END.

PLEASURE TO MEET YOU, ALEX. COULDN'T BE PROUDER TO HAVE KIN LIKE YOU.
IF YOU'D LET THE RABBIT KEEP THE BOND BETWEEN WORLDS OPEN, I WOULD BE WATCHIN' OVER YOU.
I KNOW.
BUT IT'S BETTER THIS WAY.

ALEX!

ONE MORE MINUTE, MOM!

WE'RE GONNA BE LATE.

WE WON'T BE! I PROMISE.

WHERE ARE WE EVEN GOING?

ALEX, COME ON!

YOU SURE YOU'RE FEELING OKAY? ALL HEALED UP? I CAN DRIVE IF YOU NEED.

THAT'S ACTUALLY NOT A BAD IDEA...
REALLY?!

NO.
GET IN THE CAR.

CAN I DRIVE NEXT YEAR?
IN FIVE YEARS.
FIVE?! FOUR.
SIX.
THAT'S NOT HOW NEGOTIATING WORKS!
I'M SORRY, DID YOU THINK I WAS NEGOTIATING? THESE ARE DECREES.
WHERE ARE WE EVEN GOING?

HAPPY 13th BIRTHDAY ALEX